The Marshal's Unwelcome Winter Bride

Cheryl Wright

Copyright

THE MARSHAL'S UNWELCOME WINTER BRIDE
(Unwelcome Brides Series – Book Six)

Copyright ©2025 by Cheryl Wright

Small Town Romance Publications

Dedication

To Margaret Tanner, my very dear friend and fellow author, for her enduring encouragement and friendship.

To Alan, my husband of over fifty years, who has been a relentless supporter of my writing and dreams for many years.

To You, my wonderful readers, who encourage me to continue writing these stories. It is such a joy knowing so many of you enjoy reading my stories as much as I love writing them for you.

Table of Contents

Chapter One

Langley, Montana, 1880s - Winter

Birdie Valence ran like the devil himself was chasing her.

Holding tight to her skirts she resisted the urge to check how close her pursuer was. She knew he was still there, by the grunting noises the large man made as he chased her through the snow.

She was breathless, and needed to stop, but dare not. He wasn't far behind, and Birdie couldn't risk being caught. Again.

Birdie was convinced the only reason she'd managed to escape this time was because her kidnappers decided to move her to a different location. Which suited her fine. The stench of urine and excrement was overwhelming. Why they chose the stall of a livery to keep her, Birdie would never understand.

Transporting her on a buckboard worked in Birdie's favor. She ran the moment they stopped not far from town. It was getting onto dusk, which meant she risked getting lost in the plentiful foliage, but decided it was worth the risk. Not knowing what these men had in store for her, Birdie determined it was safer to flee.

As she ran down the main street of Langley, Birdie was convinced she heard music. There was no time to stop and check it out, but the further she ran, the louder it became.

Her side was aching, and she was near breathless. If she didn't stop soon, Birdie knew she would be recaptured. This time her kidnappers would ensure she couldn't escape again. As much as they threatened to tie and gag her, they'd reneged. For that, Birdie was grateful, but knew they wouldn't be so naïve again.

The music was now booming and it was more obvious where it originated. Birdie took the opportunity to seek refuge inside the building, a church hall. Surely help would be inside? She turned the corner and slipped into the large building, then carefully pushed her way through, trying to hide in plain sight.

Still breathless, Birdie searched the crowd. It was clearly a town dance, likely arranged by the ladies auxiliary. As was the norm for these events, it appeared the entire township was in attendance. The place was packed, and there was barely room to make her way to the back of the room and out of sight. Away from harm.

As she continued to search, one man stood at least a head above everyone else. Not stopping for fear of being caught, Birdie and stared across the room at him. His eyes burned into her. His gaze stopped Birdie in her tracks. For only a moment, she'd forgotten her plight. She needed to get away, and ran to the back corner of the hall. Standing there, Birdie felt exposed. She was clearly visible to all, and that was the last thing she needed.

She felt eyes on her again. Glancing up, Birdie observed the same man who was staring at her before. This time he was frowning. He took a step toward her, which only confused Birdie. Was he going to force her to leave?

He took another few steps, then reached for her. "Are you alright?" he whispered. Without waiting for an answer, pulled her close as if they were about to dance. Except the music had now stopped.

She leaned into his chest. "Two men are trying to kidnap me," she whispered. "Again."

Birdie heard his gasp, but instead of pushing her away, as she expected, the stranger pulled her closer. She felt strangely safe in his arms.

Chapter Two

David Farris didn't know what to think. He glanced down at the woman in his arms. Her entire demeanor proved the words she said. She was rigid, not pliable as he would expect of someone who was not in danger. "What is your name?" he whispered after the initial shock wore off.

"B…Birdie," she said breathlessly.

His eyes searched the dance hall, and fell on a complete stranger. This man, he was the one chasing Birdie, David was certain. He knew every person – every child and every adult who lived in Langley. This man was a complete stranger. He was searching the room, no doubt looking for her.

David glanced about. He needed to ensure the woman was not located. Right now, she was safe with him, in his arms. He reached behind him and snatched up a grey shawl. It sat unaccompanied on a chair, and he was certain the owner would not mind. It was only for a short time, so where was the harm?

It may be the difference between life and death for Birdie.

"Hold still," he said quietly, then wrapped the borrowed shawl around her shoulders. David vowed to do everything he possibly could for this woman. He felt compelled to help the stranger in his arms.

Whether it turned out to be a bad thing was yet to be seen. Because she told him someone was trying to kidnap her, his protective side had surfaced. David hadn't felt like this in years. Not since… Nope, he wasn't going there. Instead of trying to analyze why he thought this way, his time was better spent ensuring Birdie was safe.

Moments before she arrived, he was planning to leave. He'd been there long enough to be polite, but events such as these always left him feeling…out of sorts.

Glancing up, he noticed the stranger heading their way. David guided Birdie toward the center of the dance floor, amongst the other couples. She said nothing, but glanced up in question. The stranger seemed determined to find her. "Just follow my lead," he whispered.

Moments later, he was kissing her as though Birdie was his wife and they were home alone. He heard mutterings around them, but didn't stop. Not for even a moment.

Birdie's very existence depended on it.

With his lips on hers, David felt as though he'd known her for a long time. Years. Like they were friends.

No, that was wrong. It felt as though they were husband and wife. Except the thought was ridiculous. They had met under extenuating circumstances not five minutes earlier. He carefully opened his eyes and glanced about. The stranger was still in the hall.

David's arms wrapped Birdie even tighter. "He's not far away," David whispered to her. "I need you to keep calm. I promise to keep you safe." He reached out and touched her hair. David heard Birdie's gasp as he hurriedly let her flaming auburn hair down. She stared up at him in question. "Disguise," he answered, then glanced around the room again.

He was looking for his brother, the sheriff. Garrett would help. Once the stranger was gone, or arrested, Garrett could take over.

Birdie shivered. She leaned a little closer. "There are two of them," she whispered, her voice wavering.

Two? David could only see one stranger. Where was the other man? He must be outside. No doubt guarding the door.

Finally, David spotted his brother, and signaled for him to join them. Garrett frowned. David had vowed not to get involved with any woman again. Not after… He shook himself mentally. He refused to let the memories invade his thoughts. It was long ago, but still shattered his heart.

"Everything alright here?" Garrett asked his older brother quietly. He stared at Birdie, a total stranger to them both. David felt her shudder, and held her tighter still. "See that big guy over near the door?"

Garrett glanced in the direction his brother indicated. "We don't know him?" As though realizing the man was a newcomer to town, Garrett shook his head. "Nope, we definitely don't." He stared at the man, then took a few steps toward him.

David reached out and grabbed his brother by the arm. "He is trying to kidnap this woman. I need to get her out of here." He knew his words would shock his sheriff brother, but David couldn't help it. Langley was a quiet town, and nothing ever happened here. Until tonight.

Garrett momentarily appeared bewildered, but that soon changed. He glanced about, then stared toward the large kitchen area. Before they could move, an announcement was made. "Ladies and gentlemen. The food is ready. Please, help yourselves."

The timing was perfect. While everyone surged toward the tables filled with food, David and Garrett ushered Birdie into the large kitchen. They edged her to the door in a corner of the room, which was used to bring in food for events such as this. It led out onto a small alleyway that gave sufficient cover to get Birdie out and lead her to safety.

Except now David wondered exactly what they would do with her.

Garrett hurriedly led them to the sheriff's office. He pulled down all the blinds, and locked the door. The cells were empty, as they often were, and David sat Birdie down on a chair at the sheriff's desk.

In the light of the lantern, he could see how pale the woman was. He'd assumed she was young when he stepped toward her in the low light of the dance hall. Now it was clear she was far from youthful, and appeared to be in her late thirties. He could also see she was beautiful despite being terrified.

Garrett had his pencil poised over a clean sheet of paper. "What is your name, Miss?" he asked gently.

"Birdie," she said. "Birdie Valence."

Garrett raised his eyebrows. Birdie rolled her eyes.

David had no idea what was going on. "Can someone let me in on the conspiracy?" he asked firmly.

Birdie licked her lips. "You've heard of Valence Department Stores?" She rolled her eyes again as though he was a little dense if he hadn't.

"I…I'm not sure. I think so," he added when his brother sighed.

Birdie grimaced. "My father owns them. I'm his only child, which means…"

She didn't get to finish the sentence. It suddenly hit David. "You are the sole heir."

Chapter Three

Birdie wasn't sure she did the right thing. Giving away her true identity wasn't always a good idea. Especially when people were trying to hold you for ransom.

Then again, the sheriff asked, and she needed to be truthful.

"Their names, the kidnappers that is," she said breathlessly, as though she was still running. "Are Lonnie and Hal. Apart from that, I know nothing about them." She gave her head a little shake. Birdie was still in disbelief over the entire situation.

She had been traveling in the family buggy, on her way to meet up with a friend for tea, when they were accosted. Thankfully, the driver was unharmed. At first, he'd fought back, trying to protect her. Birdie didn't want to see the man injured or worse, and demanded he cooperate.

As she recited her encounter to the sheriff and his brother, Birdie still found it hard to believe this was the reality. "I almost managed to escape from them at one point, but they caught me again." She sighed then. "They're relentless. I overheard them talking one night. They sent a ransom note to my father." With her heart pounding, Birdie felt lightheaded. "I need to let my father know I'm alive," she said firmly. Father would be terrified.

Garrett shook his head. "We can't risk sending a message to him. If it were intercepted, it would only confirm to the kidnappers where you are." He wrote on the notepad again, then studied Birdie. "Do you know those men?"

"Not at all. I've never seen them before. Not ever." As her heart continued to thump, a strange feeling came over Birdie. She needed fresh air. Birdie stood, and the room spun. The next thing she knew, she was lying on a bed in a jail cell.

David squatted down next to her and offered Birdie a glass of water. "What...? Where...?" she sputtered, not understanding how she ended up there.

"You fainted," David told her. "We decided not to get the doc because it might lead the kidnappers to you."

Her eyes scanned the cell. Garrett stood nearby as well. "What happens now?" she asked quietly. "I can't stay here. Those two will turn the town upside down looking for me."

Her gaze went from one man to the other. They stared at each other. It was clear to Birdie they knew she was right.

"We'll work something out," Garrett said. "My brother and I will come up with a plan. Right, David?"

David's eyebrows rose, and Birdie was certain he was shocked at his brother's announcement. She didn't blame him one iota. She was not his problem. He just happened to be standing alone when she needed help.

He'd gone above and beyond what she had asked of him, and Birdie couldn't fault him for that. As she studied him, Birdie noticed his features. David was tall, and quite handsome. It wasn't the thing that drew her to him though. From across the room, he seemed trustworthy. Thinking back on it now, it was a stupid thing to do. He could easily have pushed her away.

She wasn't his problem, and most men would not have lifted a finger to assist her. Instead, David guaranteed her safety, despite her being an absolute stranger to him.

At that moment, Birdie was convinced there was more to David Farris than he appeared to be.

"Of course," David said, then reached for her hand. "We'll protect you, no matter what."

His hand holding Birdie's was comforting. When he gently squeezed it, her burden felt lighter. Without saying so much as a word, he was asking her to trust him, as well as his brother. They would find a way to ensure her safety for whatever time she was here in Langley.

Birdie had always trusted people, including strangers. Now though, she was extremely cautious. She'd never felt this way before, and hated the fact her life would never be the same again.

"Thank you both," she said quietly. What else could she say? Birdie did not know this place. She'd only run into the hall because she assumed, and rightly so, the music meant there would be a large group of people congregating there. Had it been any other day of the week, she would have been captured again. Birdie knew this to be true. "If you hadn't been there…or there was no dance…" She couldn't bring herself to say the words out loud.

David squeezed her hand again. "Except none of that happened. We happened to be right where we were needed." He glanced up at the sheriff and shook his head. "You can come home with me. You'll be safe there."

Go home with a complete stranger? Her heart thudded as she thought of the ramifications. Except…what choice did she have?

He did save her life, but still… The thought of what people might think. Then again, apart from these men, she knew no one in town, so what did it matter? The most important part was being concealed from her kidnappers.

It made Birdie wonder where those horrid men were right now. Her heart pounded again, and she took some deep breaths to keep herself from panicking.

David studied her, but his expression gave nothing away. He kept his thoughts mostly to himself, but Birdie believed she could trust him. There weren't a lot of people she trusted right now, but David and the sheriff? She was convinced they would be her lifeline.

"I'll need a description of your kidnappers, when you feel up to it," Garrett told her. Birdie knew she would never feel ready to talk about those two. Except she must.

"Of course," she said, and was horrified when her stomach rumbled.

David studied her again. "When did you last eat?" he asked.

Birdie would swear the man could read her very thoughts the way he looked at her sometimes. "I'm not sure," she said cautiously, not wanting either of them to be running after her. They'd already done enough to help.

"Leave it with me," the sheriff said, then disappeared out of the cell. Birdie heard the front door open then click. For a few heartbeats, she worried the kidnappers had found her. She stiffened at the thought.

"He's gone to arrange food for you, I'm certain," David said gently as he caressed the back of her hand with his thumb.

As someone who was never upset or stressed, Birdie was annoyed. Not at David but at her kidnappers. They had turned her life upside down, and no doubt terrified her father. She stared into her rescuer's eyes. Big brown puppy dog eyes. Eyes she could get lost in had the circumstances been different. "I don't want to be a bother," she said firmly. Or at least as firmly as she could manage at this point.

It wasn't long before Birdie heard a key turn in the lock, then the door firmly closed. Moments later, Garrett appeared with a plate piled high with food.

As though on cue, her stomach rumbled again. This time, David chuckled.

Chapter Four

The last thing David wanted to do was embarrass Birdie. Except he couldn't help but chuckle. It was as though her stomach was rumbling in sync with Garrett's appearance. He watched as she stared at the plate of food she desperately craved.

Helping her sit up, David took the plate Garrett offered. "Why don't you get Birdie a cup of tea?" David suggested. His eyes were suddenly drawn to her dry and cracked lips. Not only had she been kidnapped, but Birdie had been completely neglected.

As well as being starved, she'd been left without water. His eyes went to her hands. They too, were cracked. Left much longer that way, they would no doubt be painful. He might not want the doc to come here to the sheriff's office, but once he had Birdie safely tucked away, there was no reason for anyone to suspect she was there.

By anyone, he meant her kidnappers. His heart thudded at the thought of somebody wanting to hurt this fragile woman.

David hoped they'd already left town. Knowing she was their source of income, it was highly unlikely. "Do you feel like staying here or moving to the sheriff's desk?" The beds were not the most comfortable, and he didn't want her to suffer any further discomfort.

"I'm fine here," she said, staring longingly at the food he held.

Now he was annoyed at himself. He pushed the plate toward her, and Birdie reached for slice of egg and ham pie. Her hands shook, and she had trouble picking it up. Wrapping his hand gently around hers, David knew he was already too deeply involved in Birdie's dilemma.

She glanced up at him, and for the first time, he stared into her face. Despite all the angst she'd suffered, and the torture she'd endured, Birdie was beautiful. He helped her bring the pie to her mouth, and watched her expression change as she took a small bite of the food.

It broke his heart to think of the treatment she'd endured. Kidnapping someone was bad enough, but starving them was beyond the realms of decency.

Little by little, Birdie ate the entire slice of pie. It wasn't much, but it was probably more than enough for now. If she'd been without sustenance for some days, and it appeared she had, eating too much at once could do more harm than good. He handed off the plate with its remaining food to his brother.

Garrett seemed as concerned about their guest as David was. They both knew the situation was risky for all of them. And yet, neither man cared. Their only concern was for Birdie. His eyes strayed from his brother back to Birdie. She was barely staying awake. "Why don't you rest for a while?" he asked. When she nodded, David helped her to lie down, then covered her with a blanket.

Unlike Garrett's prisoners, he wanted Birdie to be comfortable, and to feel protected. Where she was at this moment, she was safe, and both he and his brother would look after her. David desperately wanted to capture her kidnappers, but Birdie had to be his priority.

As though his sheriff brother could read his mind, Garrett touched his shoulder and indicated for David to follow him out of the cell. He glanced down at Birdie. She was already sound asleep, and would likely stay that way for some time.

"She needs medical treatment," David whispered, endeavoring to not wake Birdie. Despite his words, he knew bringing the doc here this late at night would raise suspicions. Especially with it being dance night. Most of the townsfolk were in attendance. Bringing attention to the sheriff's office would raise suspicion. Especially if the kidnappers were still hanging around. There was no doubt in David's mind they were in town. From the little he knew, Birdie was worth too much in ransom money for them to simply walk away.

"My deputy will be here shortly. We can do a thorough search, if you can stay here." Garrett already stood and headed to the window. Pulling the coverings aside, he glanced into the darkness. "I can't see anyone loitering around, but that means nothing. It won't be long and the dance will be finished. Most people will leave at the same time, making it even more difficult to find the abductors."

Garrett was right and they both knew it. Sitting here doing nothing was wrong. David wanted to get out there and arrest those cruel and uncaring men. Only *he* couldn't. But if he found them, it would be a different story. David glanced down at his marshal's badge. He was certain Birdie had not realized he was a lawman. It was simply luck she'd chosen him to get help.

Except he was on temporary leave – at his own choosing.

Without warning the door handle rattled. David's heart rate increased, and he gasped. "It's Virgil. Deputy Collins," the man called through the door. David's relief was palpable. Garrett hurried to the door and let his deputy inside. "What's going on?"

Virgil asked, his gaze moving from one man to the other.

"We have a situation," Garrett told him.

The three men sat around the sheriff's desk and decided on a strategy. One that would keep Birdie safe.

~*~

David locked the door to the sheriff's office the moment the two lawmen left. They would systematically check every building, the livery, the church, and anywhere else Birdie's assailants could hide. He pulled his gun from its holster and checked the chamber, reassuring himself he was ready for anything.

It had been a while since he'd fired a gun, but wasn't averse to doing so if it meant saving the sleeping woman. The moment their eyes met across the room, he knew she was in trouble. He'd been a lawman for far too long. He knew what desperation looked like.

Langley was a friendly town. Quiet most of the time, and some folks found it too quiet. Is that why the kidnappers came here? Did they believe they would just blend in and get away with their crimes? Or were they merely passing through when their victim escaped?

It told David a lot about Birdie. She had stamina, and far more backbone than most men he knew. He sipped the strong black coffee he'd poured the moment the sheriff and his deputy left. Not that he was particularly tired – the events of the night had him wide awake and on alert. But a man could never be sure.

David would be ready for anything. Even if that meant killing a man to save Birdie – the stranger who had already stolen his heart.

Chapter Five

Birdie awoke with a start. She lay still as she listened to her surroundings.

The door. The sound she heard was the click of the front door locking. She breathed a sigh of relief.

Until she believed she was now alone in the sheriff's office. Sitting up slowly, Birdie put her feet to the floor. She made as little sound as possible, in case Lonnie and Hal, her kidnappers, were here.

Her heart pounded, and she lamented the fact she had no firearm. Nor did she have access to anything to protect herself with. Birdie glanced about – nothing of any use as a weapon caught her eye. She had nothing more than her boots. They could hurt if thrown hard enough, but against a gun were useless.

Instead of calming herself, Birdie panicked. That both David and Garrett left her alone was beyond belief. Why would they do that?

It was then she realized it may not be the case. She had concocted a scenario in her mind, and gone with it. After all she'd been through, Birdie wasn't surprised.

She didn't know David well, barely at all if she was truthful, but sensed he wasn't the type to abandon a woman in need of protection.

She didn't know what it was about him, but David seemed to be the protective type. He ensured she was not seen by her kidnappers at the dance, and got her out of there. All without her being revealed. It told her a lot about the man.

Now, in her stockinged feet, Birdie crept out of the cell and toward the front of the sheriff's office. It's where the sound had originated. Her heart thudded in her chest, and she was more scared than she'd ever been in her life. Except perhaps when she was snatched. She needed to know what or who she was dealing with.

The intruder had his back to her, and had made himself at home sitting at the sheriff's desk. It wasn't the sheriff, she was certain.

The man was drinking coffee, and Birdie couldn't get over the cheek of the man.

She held a boot in each hand, and was ready to throw them when he glanced over his shoulder. "Ah, you're awake," David said with a smile. "I hope it helped." He stood, then stared at the boots she held tightly, ready to use as weapons.

Then he chuckled. He didn't say a word, didn't need to. David knew exactly what she had planned, and found it laughable.

Birdie quickly hid the boots behind her back as she felt heat rise in her cheeks. What he thought of her, Birdie didn't want to know.

Without so much as a word, David led her to a chair at the sheriff's desk. "Tea or coffee?" he asked. Birdie was expecting him to denigrate her, or at the very least make a comment about the boots she was attempting to hide. But he didn't.

She studied him. He was a man of the world, she was certain. She guessed David was in his early forties. It meant he had to have been around. She couldn't begin to imagine the experiences he'd had.

Unlike herself. She had lived all her life in Helena, although she'd been on several vacations with her parents. After Mother had died, neither Birdie nor Father felt like enjoying themselves on holidays that didn't include her mother.

It hadn't taken long for would-be suitors to call, but she put up a wall, and refused their attentions. As a result, her experience of the world was narrow. Limited. More's the pity.

Birdie was now aware of David staring at her. "Are you alright?" he asked gently, then reached out for her hands. But they were behind her back.

She let the boots drop to the floor and he chuckled again. Did the man find her discomfort amusing? It certainly appeared that way.

The moment her hands were free, she put them in front of her, allowing David to hold them. Why she even contemplated it, she had no idea. Except for the fact he made her feel comforted and protected.

He glanced first at her hands, then his gaze moved to the boots lying on the floor behind her. He tried stifling a chuckle, but failed miserably. At first Birdie glared at him. Then she couldn't help but join in. He continued to hold both her hands. Moments later, he was staring into her face as Birdie continued to laugh.

David suddenly let go of her hands. He reached out and wiped her cheeks. Confusion filled her.

"Birdie," he said gently, then pulled her close, wrapping her in his arms. It was then she saw his shirt was wet. But only where her face leaned against him. "We will catch those men and arrest them. I promise."

His hand caressed her cheek, and Birdie glanced up into his face. He seemed to truly care about her, which was both nice and equally confusing. They had only known each other for a matter of hours.

Sipping the tea David made for her, Birdie was feeling more calm. Without knowing the reason, she trusted him implicitly. It wasn't due to his brother being a sheriff, she felt certain. She couldn't quite put her finger on it, and frankly, she didn't have the energy at this moment to ponder the answer further.

He strolled across the room and returned with the plate of food his brother had retrieved earlier. Birdie was hungry. She was also afraid to eat in case it made her ill. Apart from the food she ate in the cell earlier, she'd been deprived of food since her abduction. She couldn't be certain, but was convinced that was three, maybe four days ago.

The truth was, being deprived of sustenance was probably a godsend. Her kidnappers had no care for her well-being, and provided nothing in the way of facilities. She was still wearing the clothing she was snatched in.

She turned her head and sniffed. It wasn't pleasant and caused her to scowl.

Out of the corner of her eye, she noticed David staring at her. "Is everything alright?" he asked. Birdie knew he wasn't being nosey, but was concerned for her.

She shook her head. "I stink," she whispered. "They kept me in a livery stall most of the time." She glanced up and noticed the fury covering his face. "I am wearing the same clothes I wore when they…" Birdie swallowed down her emotions. She didn't want to say the words out loud.

David's hand snaked across the table and covered her hands. He was so gentle. So incredibly caring. It caused her eyes to fill with tears. Except she didn't know why. He shuffled his chair closer to hers and embraced her. "It will all work out," he said gently. "I'm not sure when it will be, but I'll arrange a bath for you, and clean clothes." He squeezed her hands, then spoke again. "I promise to protect you, no matter what."

Tears again sprung from her eyes and trickled down her cheeks. Birdie couldn't believe her luck. David was the man she needed to help her. How she had chosen him to go to for help, she may never truly know. The reason she'd gravitated to him? His eyes. They were kind and caring. He'd stared at her from across the room. He took the time to check if she was alright or in some sort of trouble.

Out of everyone at the dance, David was the only person there who saw her for what she was. A woman in distress who needed protection.

Chapter Six

David knew he couldn't let himself get involved with this woman. This stranger whose life was in peril.

He didn't want to get caught up in whatever it was she'd found herself entangled in. Except he couldn't walk away. Birdie had no idea who or what he was, and yet she had trusted him. It had only been a matter of hours since they'd met, and already he felt a deep connection to her. If he revealed his occupation to her, how would she feel, he wondered.

It was bound to come out soon, so he might as well tell her. He opened his mouth to speak, but his heart thudded. David had no idea why it was the case. Glancing down into her face, he couldn't help but notice her fear. Would telling her make Birdie feel better? He could only believe it would.

"Birdie," he said, then took a sip of coffee to moisten his dry mouth. David did not know why it was the case. He had nothing to hide. He would do right by this woman who had been held captive and deprived of her basic human rights. Glancing into her face, he saw her curiosity. "I have to tell you something." The color quickly drained from her face. "It's not bad, I promise," he said, and squeezed her hands again.

For someone in her situation, it could only be a relief, right? Of course he was right, he knew he was. And yet he still felt apprehensive. "That's good," she said, but her face was still pale. "I don't think I could take anymore bad news."

She glanced down at their entwined hands, then back to his face. Instead of removing his hands as David knew he should, he lifted her hands and brought them closer to him. He instinctively wanted to kiss them, but held back. It was the right thing to do. He sighed. "I need to tell you…"

At that moment, the door rattled. David reached for his gun, and pointed it in the direction of the door. He shoved Birdie behind him, all the while keeping his aim toward the door. Apart from the door that led into the courthouse, there was only one way in and out of the sheriff's office.

Deputy Collins was the first inside, followed by David's brother. He kept his gun trained on the door, in case the kidnappers were nearby. The moment the door was closed and locked, his gun was returned to its holster.

"All clear," Garrett said. "We've searched high and low, and can't find anyone who doesn't belong in town.

"Did you find their buckboard?" Birdie asked quietly. She needed to know if they were still around. David could understand that. "It was not far outside the town boundary – on the edge of it, I guess."

David stared at his brother, silently asking the question. Garrett answered with a discreet shake of his head. David sighed.

What they would do now, David wasn't sure. What he did know was first light, there would be another search. This one more thorough. He wasn't blaming Garrett or his deputy. It was pitch black outside. The only light came from the moon. There was only so much one could do in that situation.

In the meantime, they needed to make some decisions about Birdie. Where would she sleep tonight? And how would they get her away from the sheriff's office without being seen? Both those questions needed to be answered, and soon.

"If you can't find them, does that mean Lonnie and Hal have left town?" Birdie's eyes seemed to plead with him to say it was true. Except David couldn't lie to her. She deserved the truth.

"Not necessarily," he said gently as he guided her back into the chair she previously occupied. He pushed the plate of food toward her again, and set about refilling her cup with tea. "They don't know where you are, and won't get anywhere near you," David said. "That's a promise."

Despite nodding acceptance of his words, Birdie's expression didn't change. She appeared as worried now as she did ten minutes ago. He knew they needed to get her out of here and away from town, but how they managed to do it without her being seen was the question.

David's head pounded. He needed sleep, but so did Birdie. In his line of work, there were times he was awake for almost two days. It wasn't the best situation, but often couldn't be helped. Except he was older now, and wasn't the young buck of twenty years ago. If he could get her out of here unseen, he was certain his headache would decrease to an acceptable and more bearable level.

The coffee was hot and strong, and David filled three mugs with it. It wouldn't help the pounding in his head, but it might assist in forming a plan. He watched Birdie as she nibbled on a cookie and sipped her tea. Then she pushed the plate to the center of the desk. "I've had enough. Help yourselves," she told no one in particular. It was then she stood. "I'm going to lay down, if you don't mind," she added, then headed toward the cells.

Standing when Birdie did, David followed her, despite her protests. "I'll make sure you're settled," he told her, and she nodded.

He almost chuckled when he noticed the boots in her hands. Despite her dire situation, and the absurdity of her plan to attack using those boots, she didn't try to hide them from him.

She laid down on the narrow bed, and was asleep almost the moment her head hit the lumpy pillow. It was cold in the cells, there was no doubting it. David gently covered her with a blanket, and stared down at the woman he'd rescued from certain death. She might have survived this long, but he knew from experience most hostages did not live once the ransom was paid. Birdie would have been a loose end the kidnappers had to tie up.

His heart thudded at the thought. The question now was how did he get her out of the sheriff's office and to somewhere safe? He lifted his head as he pondered the question. The answer hit David in the face.

"Do you honestly think we'll get away with it?" Garrett, David's brother and Langley's sheriff, didn't seem so certain. "You want to do this in broad daylight? Are you crazy?" Garrett shook his head and glanced at his deputy.

Virgil didn't say anything for a bit, and David knew the deputy was pondering the scenario. Suddenly the deputy nodded his head enthusiastically. "I do believe it could work. It will take some serious planning, but we can pull it off."

There was nothing to be done until daylight. They needed supplies from the mercantile, and had to also wait for the livery to open. The entire operation would be a delicate one, but David was convinced, provided everyone did their part, it was highly possible they'd get away with it.

"I'm making more coffee," he announced. "I can't stay awake much longer."

Deputy Virgil Collins stood. "Why don't you both get some sleep? I'll let you know if I need you."

David began to grumble, but knew Virgil was right. Either way, Virgil would be here and awake. He always did the night shift, so would be wide awake. The brothers made their way to the cells where Birdie slept soundly. They kept as quiet as they possibly could, and lay down on the uncomfortable beds. Certain he wouldn't sleep, David lay there, his eyes closed. He was soon fast asleep, and didn't wake until Virgil shook his shoulder several hours later.

"Shhh," Virgil said quietly, a finger to his lip. "The mercantile is open." He turned away then and repeated the process with Garrett.

Glancing across at Birdie, David noticed she was still sound asleep. She obviously needed the rest, and they didn't need her yet. He'd let her sleep until the last minute.

He stepped outside, and waited until the door was secured behind him. Then he strolled across the road to the mercantile. He saw the bakery was open, and decided to call in there on the way back. They would all need sustenance.

He conducted his business at the mercantile as quickly as possible, buying food supplies as well. Calling into the bakery took far less time, but was equally important as far as David was concerned.

Outside the sheriff's office again, he knocked and called out, identifying himself. He had been ever vigilant, watching for strangers and strange buggies. None were noticed.

Once inside, he put the box of groceries aside. They would be needed over the next few days as he kept Birdie safe. He bought far more than he anticipated they'd need, but knew it was better to be safe than sorry.

It was only moments later Birdie strolled out of the cells, her feet bare. She was rubbing her eyes, and her hair was a mess, but she still looked beautiful to David.

He knew then he was in big trouble. Not from the kidnappers, but his reaction to Birdie Valence.

Chapter Seven

Birdie glanced about. Something was afoot, but she couldn't work out what was going on. There was an excitement in the room, and the atmosphere was palpable. When she went to bed last night, it was more like doom and gloom.

What happened to change everyone's mood?

"Good morning," she said, glancing from one man to the other. "You all seem happy this morning." She cocked her head to the side and stared at David. She watched as he wriggled under her intense scrutiny.

Instead of questioning her, he made her a cup of tea and placed it on the desk. "I've been to the bakery. This is for you," he said, handing her a still-warm pastry.

"What about the rest of you?" she demanded. She couldn't eat if they didn't.

A smile crossed his face. "We've already eaten. They were fresh out of the oven when I bought them."

Birdie lifted the pastry to her lips and took a tentative bite. "Delicious," she said, then took another bite. She'd never eaten anything so tasty. The delicacy finished, she drank down the tea David made for her.

Without another word, she glanced from one man to the next. There was nervous energy filling the room. But why?

Something was going on. Of that she was certain.

"Birdie," David said, his expression one she couldn't decipher. "We have a plan." He ushered her into the cell where she'd slept. She glanced up at him, raising her eyebrows. In response, he studied her, then placed some items on the bed. She couldn't discern what they were, but they looked suspiciously like men's clothing.

She leaned down and picked them up. There was a plaid shirt, a jacket, men's pants, a pair of socks, and men's underwear. There was also a cowboy hat.

Curious.

Her mouth opened, Birdie was about to ask what was going on, when she heard the front door open and lock again. It got more curious by the minute.

"What is your plan?" she demanded, annoyed she hadn't been included in this plan of theirs.

David shuffled his feet. "You will dress as a man. The hat is to cover up your hair, so make sure it is well tucked up underneath." Turning away from her, he walked away. "I'll leave you alone. Come into the office when you are ready."

"Men's underwear, really?" she said, annoyed as she studied the item.

"We couldn't arouse suspicion," David told her, his cheeks pink with embarrassment.

Her head spinning, Birdie stood looking down at the assortment laying on top of the bed. "Whatever are they up to?" she said out loud, knowing full well she was the only person who would hear.

She undressed from the putrid clothes she wore, dropping them on the floor. A bath would go down well right now, but it was something that would put her life in further danger. It was obvious she was being moved, but why was she to dress as a man? It was certainly confusing.

Birdie stripped down until she was almost naked, her corset being the only item she kept. Shaking her head in confusion, she pulled on the men's underpants, which didn't fit well, as she'd already surmised would be the case. The shirt at least looked as though it may be a better fit, and as it turned out it was.

"We're almost ready for you, Birdie," David called from the other room. "Are you decent?"

"No!" she shouted. "Do *not* come in here!" David's chuckle made its way to her, which irritated Birdie even more. She quickly finished dressing, and tucked her hair up under the hat, which was far too big. If only she had some hair clips to hold her long hair in place.

As she pulled her boots on over the socks, Birdie heard the click of the door. A shudder went through her, despite knowing she was protected by three men. Two of whom were lawman.

Moments later, she cautiously ventured out into the sheriff's office, in case the door was still open. It wasn't, but the three men stood in a huddle. They were talking quietly, and it was clear their aim was to ensure she didn't hear the discussion.

"I'm ready," she said loud enough to make them all turn around and stare at her. "Do I look manly enough for you?" She raised her eyebrows at the three men, who stared at her. David seemed to study her more closely, but finally a grin came to his face.

Stepping toward her, he carefully checked her over. "May I?" he asked, pointing toward the hat. "Your hair needs fixing."

As much as Birdie felt exasperated, she had no mirror to see what she was doing, and was grateful to let David help. "This hat is far too big," he said more to himself than anyone else. "I'll be back shortly," he said, taking the hat with him.

True to his words, he was gone a short time. He returned carrying a smaller sized cowboy hat. "This should fit better," he announced, and fiddled with her hair again. Birdie had no idea why, but a shiver went down her spine while he fixed her hair. "That's much better," he announced. "It's time to leave," he said, then walked toward the cells.

Birdie followed, along with the two lawman, but had no idea where they were going. Curiosity finally got the better of her, and she needed to know. "Where…where are we going?" she asked warily. David opened the door in front of them, and Birdie immediately saw the short tunnel. Fear filled her.

She had believed these men were going to protect her, but now?

Now, she was uncertain.

David turned to face her. "We're going into the courthouse. We have a paddy wagon waiting outside." He opened the door at the other end of the small tunnel, while Birdie tried to take it all in. "I can see you're confused," he said. "We are going to make it look as though you are a prisoner being taken from Langley to prison. Hence the men's clothing."

She breathed a sigh of relief, then the obvious hit her. "We're doing this in broad daylight?"

"That's when we usually transport prisoners," the sheriff told her. "It won't be out of place." He nodded at David, and they continued to move out of the tunnel, and toward the front door. "You will now be held by the sheriff and the deputy," he said. "They'll place you in the wagon, and Deputy Collins will drive you out of town."

Her head spinning, Birdie had no choice but to agree. Where they planned to take her after that, Birdie had no idea. So far they seemed to know what they were doing. Whether it worked was another question all together. Her biggest fear was these men were risking their lives for her. There was no way she could ever repay them.

Chapter Eight

David waited around half an hour before heading to the livery. He needed to give Virgil and Birdie enough time to leave town, and not rouse suspicion.

Shoving his hat on his head, David glanced about. There were few people around, and definitely no strangers. As far as he could tell, the kidnappers had not left town. It meant they were still here somewhere. It did not appease David's fears for Birdie.

"Be careful," his brother Garrett said as David left the sheriff's office.

David stared momentarily at his brother, then the two men embraced. This entire scenario would be difficult. He hadn't visited for quite a while. His heart thudded at the very thought.

"I'll be fine," David said. His words sounded far more certain than he felt.

On his way to collect his horse, David stopped at the telegraph office. His message was already written and ready to go. He had to be careful to ensure it didn't get into the wrong hands, but even if it did, his cryptic words would mean nothing to most people.

The ride to the ranch alone was not exactly what he'd hoped for. David's thoughts were all over the place. It had been a while, and his heart thudded the moment the ranch came into view.

He could do this, he knew he could.

There was no sign of the paddy wagon when he arrived, but the barn doors were wide open. That told him the wagon was in the barn, hiding from any prying eyes.

David slowed his horse, then dismounted close to the house. His heart pounded as he glanced about. Memories came flooding back, and not all of them welcomed. Climbing the steps to the ranch house was one of the hardest things he'd done for a long time.

Virgil met him at the top of the steps. "How are you doing?" he asked.

David simply shook his head. He'd know from the moment he suggested they come here it would be tough. Glancing past Virgil's shoulder he could see Birdie. She sat quietly on the sofa, the dust covers still in place.

She stood the second she saw him. "Why am I here?" she asked, her voice full of confusion. And perhaps even laced with fear.

Instead of answering as he knew he should, David glanced about. He reached out and grabbed Birdie's hand, then set about going from room to room. "Here's the kitchen," he said, then moved to the pantry. It needed no explanation except the fact most of the items here would be ruined.

"Ew, weevils," she said as she opened the container of flour.

"I'll get rid of those," David said, then took her back to the sitting room. "There's a root cellar back there." He pointed, and Birdie nodded. "We will remove all the coverings. The furniture should still be in good condition." He didn't provide an explanation, and wondered how long it would take Birdie to ask.

He led her to the master bedroom next. David walked over to the bed and picked up the closest pillow. He brought it to his face and breathed in. He glanced briefly at Birdie. Her confusion was clear.

Placing the pillow back where it belonged, he opened the closet. "Take your pick of clothes," he said gently. "They should fit. You're about the same size." He ran his fingers along the quilt covering the double bed, but didn't say a word. His heart was breaking all over again. He reached for Birdie's hand, and led her to the next room. "The rest of these rooms are unused," he said, his voice breaking as he stood in the doorway. The closet was exactly where he'd left it, and the small bassinette…

His heart thudded in that moment. If he didn't get out of here, his emotions would overtake him. Instead of explaining, he turned and strolled out of the room without another word.

He needed fresh air. Not that it would take away his pain, but maybe, just maybe the cold air might make him feel a little better.

David knew Birdie would be confused by his behavior, but right now, his heart was breaking all over again.

Virgil glanced at him as David stormed outside. Despite snow and the cold, he welcomed the fresh air.

Too late now, but he should have insisted Garrett came instead of his deputy. His brother had always been there to support him, and although Virgil knew what happened, it wasn't the same.

He sat on the steps to the porch, and breathed deeply. It wasn't enough. Instead, he stood and walked over to the closest field. It's emptiness hit him equally hard. His plan had always been to come back here and continue his life. Except David didn't know how to do that. Not after everything had gone so terribly wrong.

He heard footsteps behind him and spun around, his hand on his gun. Relief filled him at the sight of Birdie. No more did she wear the men's clothes, but one of the pretty gowns that were going to waste. The gowns he didn't have the heart to give away.

"You need to stay inside," he heard Virgil say.

He studied Birdie. She was determined, he would give her that. Except David believed she didn't know what she'd gotten herself into. Not that any of it was her fault. She was born into this predicament, so how could she be to blame?

Virgil climbed down the steps and headed toward David, who still stood at the fence. "We had a large herd of horses," he said quietly. "It's strange to come here and not see them." He turned his head away and wiped at a tear that was making its way down his cheek.

"Are you alright, David?" Virgil asked gently. "This can't be easy for you." He slapped a hand to David's back, then pulled the other man in to embrace him.

"I'll be alright. It's just…difficult…as I knew it would be." He turned back to face the house. "Guess I'd best get on with it," he said, then strolled across the yard with determination, and entered the sitting room. He then removed all the dust covers.

He sat down for a few minutes, simply contemplating. Then he stood and went outside again. They needed wood for the fires, and it wasn't going to cut itself.

After retrieving an axe from the barn, he began to chop wood. Everything was exactly as he'd left it. He wasn't certain, but perhaps it was the reason his heart was breaking. Coming back here after so long, he'd hoped it had changed. Of course, he knew it wouldn't be the case. How could it? The ranch house had been locked up and unused since…

He ran a hand across his forehead. It wasn't hot, far from it, but there were beads of sweat he needed to wipe away. Glancing up, he glimpsed Birdie. She'd pulled the window coverings back slightly, and was watching him.

Moments later, she was gone.

David stayed outside until he was satisfied with the amount of wood he'd chopped. He hoped they wouldn't be here long – his heart couldn't take it. It wasn't long before he went inside carrying a large box of logs for the fire.

Building a fire would give him something to do. God knew he needed a distraction, and this was it. Squatting down at the fireplace brought it's own set of memories. He glanced over his shoulder. Birdie sat waiting. For him?

David wasn't sure.

He owed her the truth, but wasn't sure he could say the words. His entire life changed in that short time three years ago. David hadn't been the same man ever since.

Chapter Nine

Birdie could see David's pain. It was written all over his face. When he'd taken her to the main bedroom, it was clear – he'd lost someone close to him.

When he stood outside the next bedroom, it all became very clear.

Her heart broke as she studied the unused bassinette. Nearby was an open closet. In it was a variety of baby clothes. Birdie glanced down at the gown she was wearing. They must have belonged to someone he loved. Likely his wife.

No wonder he was subdued. It was now clear to Birdie he was a widower. Did his wife and child die in childbirth? She didn't picture him as man who would abandon his family. Besides, the furniture in the two bedrooms she visited told her otherwise.

He squatted down at the fireplace and prepared it to light a fire. She came down to his level, and glanced at him. "I'm so sorry, David. We can leave here if you prefer. And I'll change. I assume these are her clothes." The last thing she wanted to do was hurt the man who saved her from those awful men.

He shook his head then went back to the task at hand. Perhaps it was better to leave him alone with his thoughts. She would wander about, and find everything she needed. "Did the groceries come inside yet?" she asked Virgil. "I haven't seen them."

"They're still in the wagon. I'll fetch them," he said, then left the house quietly. Birdie reached up into one of the overhead cupboards. Everything was dusty. She would have to wash every plate, every mug, and anything else that had sat here since David had abandoned his home.

She rummaged through all the cupboards and emptied them as she went. Once the woodstove had a fire under it and was hot, she could make coffee. She would also have to think about meals. Birdie had no idea what supplies David had bought, but hopefully there was enough for her to make a decent meal.

She went into the pantry once more, and did a more thorough check. Anything that had weevils was dumped in an empty box. She opened the icebox and breathed a sigh of relief to find it empty. Birdie hoped she could say the same about the root cellar.

One thing at a time, she told herself. It doesn't all have to be done in one day. Except keeping busy was also keeping her sane. Being pursued by kidnappers was not her idea of fun. Not on any level.

The outbreak of weevils indicated the ranch house had been empty for quite some time. It had her pondering how long it was since David had lost his family. A few months? A year. Or perhaps far longer.

She did not want to add to his pain, and would again suggest they leave here. Except the timing had to be right. Today was not the time to do so. She was convinced of it.

Returning to the kitchen with the box of contaminated products, she found David lighting the woodstove. He glanced at her, but didn't say a word. Birdie would leave him with his thoughts, although if he was anything like her, his mind would be working overtime.

She carried the box with the evil critters outside. "Weevils," she told Virgil, and he directed her to an empty drum not far from the house.

"On second thought," he said, "let me. You shouldn't be out here."

He was probably right. As far as anyone knew, they weren't followed. They hoped Lonnie and Hal had left the area, but there was no proof they had.

Virgil took the box from her hands. It wasn't heavy, but it felt like a weight had been lifted from her shoulders. Birdie wasn't sure why, especially knowing David's situation. One thing she knew, Birdie wouldn't bring it up again, except to offer to leave. Once she'd done that for a second time, it would be the end of the discussion. His pain was her pain. Her heart felt as though it had shattered.

She barely knew this man, but knew he was kind and caring. Until now, she hadn't known he was heartbroken as well.

~*~

"Lunch was delicious," Virgil said as he finished up the last of the pancakes. "Those fried potatoes and onions finished them off nicely.

David glanced across at him. "I agree. Birdie is an excellent cook." He studied her, then continued. "I didn't think you would know how. Coming from a wealthy background."

Birdie rolled her eyes. "There was just Father and myself after my mother died. I saw no point wasting money on a cook." She took a sip of tea, before continuing. "I'm not the best cook around, but I *can* put together a decent meal."

David nodded, but said nothing.

Virgil also nodded. "Well, from where I sit, you put together a more than decent meal. Best I've had for a long time."

"You must be cooking for yourself," David joked, and Virgil smiled.

"Can't go to the diner much. Not on deputy wages." He glanced down at his pocket watch. "I will be off soon. It's been enough time to get to the prison, with a little dallying time." He drank down the last of his coffee then stood.

"There's pie," Birdie said. She sounded desperate even to her own ears. Was she worried about being here alone with David? It had nothing to do with protection, she knew. But what did it mean?

Virgil grinned and took his place at the table once more. Birdie dished out apple pie for everyone. David had purchased cream, so they could splurge with it, but it wouldn't last long. The same could be said for all the supplies.

After today she would need to be frugal with everything. At least David had purchased staple items. She would have to think hard for each meal. They couldn't afford to run out of supplies before they could leave here.

Birdie glanced about. She liked this place. Apart from feeling safe and comfortable, it was peaceful. It was already beginning to feel like home.

It was the last thing she wanted. Home was in Helena, not out in the back woods of Langley. And not with strangers who held her life in their hands.

Chapter Ten

David was beginning to settle back into life on the ranch, although something was missing, and he wasn't talking about animals. When he'd left three years ago, Garrett had taken care of everything for him.

The one thing he hadn't done was remove all evidence of David's family from the house. Garrett told him it wasn't healthy to simply pretend they never existed.

He knew Garrett was right, but today was painful. His heart was breaking all over again. Birdie, intelligent woman that she was, worked it out quickly.

"Are you going to be alright?" Virgil asked. "Should I send Garrett out here?"

He was tempted to say yes, but Garrett had work to do. David wouldn't interfere with his sheriff duties. Especially knowing there could still be kidnappers lurking about. "I'll be fine. We'll be fine," he said, hoping above all else it was true.

Virgil climbed up onto the wagon. The horses had all been brushed and watered, and well fed. The trip was little more than an hour from town, but David always ensured his horses were well cared for. His own horse stood alone in the barn right now, but he would let him out into the field once Virgil was gone.

It would be good to see some semblance of normality again. After all this was over, he would think about restocking the ranch. *If he decided to stay.*

It meant he would have to move back home. He was certain Garrett would be pleased to be rid of him.

His brother had been his lifeline. David had not coped well with Mae's death. Or the loss of their baby. His son had been stillborn, which was heartbreaking in itself. His wife lingered for a few hours, but it was made clear to him by the doc, she wouldn't make it.

It was then he knew he'd have to leave. Except David believed he would return after a few days or weeks at most. Perhaps after the funeral.

He simply couldn't bring himself to do it.

Being back here brought up all the emotions of that day. Birdie's offer to leave had tempted him, but he couldn't do it to her. Besides, he had to move on.

Mae wouldn't want him to stop living, which is exactly what he'd done.

Watching the wagon disappear down the long drive and out of sight, David knew it wouldn't be easy staying here, but he would do it, and he would survive it. More importantly, Birdie would be safe.

After glancing across the vast property he owned, David turned and headed back inside. Birdie stood in the doorway watching him. He wondered what was going through her mind. Garrett suggested David tell her while they were still in town, but he decided against it. She needed a safe place to stay, and even with the little he knew about her, David was certain she would refuse to come here.

She seemed concerned about the feelings of others. She'd already proven it by asking if he wanted to go back to town.

"Are you alright?" she asked, proving his point.

He nodded. There was no way David would admit her concern for him had his emotions all over the place.

He needed to tell Birdie what he'd already tried to say once before, but was interrupted. How she would take it, he didn't know, but the truth was the only way to go.

~*~

The aroma coming from the kitchen was enticing. He missed the days of home-cooked meals. He and Garrett took turns to cook, but some nights they simply gave in and went to the diner. They were there more often than not.

David knew he could quickly get used to Birdie's cooking. He was already endeared to the woman herself, but knew he shouldn't be. Especially here where Mae's presence could be felt everywhere he looked.

"Sit down," Birdie demanded. "The muffins are hot and ready for eating." She'd already placed a fresh coffee on the table for him. Birdie was bending over backwards to try and have him feel at home. What's more, it was working.

"Birdie," he said as he dragged a chair out from the table. "I have something important to tell you." She placed a plate of muffins in front of him. He waited until she was seated before he spoke again. He watched as she chewed on her bottom lip. He'd scared her. "It's nothing terrible. At least I don't think it is." He reached for a muffin and put it on the small plate she'd put there for him. "They really are hot," he said, trying to avoid the inevitable. She sat staring at him, waiting for him to confess. "I should have told you long ago," he said quietly. "And I did try at the sheriff's office, but we were interrupted."

"How bad is it?" she asked, her sad blue eyes never leaving his.

David knew he was putting it off with every word he spoke. He reached for his coffee, and wrapped his hands around the mug and lifted it to his lips. "I'm a marshal," he said gently, then took a huge mouthful of the hot beverage. "At least I was."

Birdie's sigh had him wondering what she'd expected him to say. "But you're not now?" She seemed confused.

"Strictly speaking, I'm still a marshal," he said. The muffins were cooler now and he took a bite. "This is good," he said, then bit into it again. Birdie stared at him. She seemed to be waiting for him to continue. "When…" He swallowed hard. "After…after the funeral, I went on indefinite leave."

"And you never went back," she finished for him. "Why not?"

David was certain she knew the reason, but she wanted him to admit it for himself. It was something he wasn't good at doing. "I couldn't face life without Mae and the baby."

"Yet, you came here today. It took a lot of courage for you to come back. Especially with all the ghosts of your past." She reached across the table and held his hand with her own. David didn't say a word. He knew it was wrong, but he let her comfort him anyway.

David was adamant he did not want a relationship of any kind. It wasn't like Birdie was offering him one, but he needed to get his mind straight. Living in close proximity as they would over the next few days, they were bound to be drawn to each other.

It made him wonder if Birdie felt the same way. He would keep his distance as much as possible, but feared it was already too late. At least now Birdie understood his situation, and was likely to ensure they didn't get close.

He owed it to Mae. David had told his wife on her deathbed, he would never fall in love again or remarry. Her response had him reeling.

Chapter Eleven

Birdie had no idea why she'd reached out to David.

It was clear he was hurting, but like most men, tried to hide his feelings. Standing in the doorway to the main bedroom, watching him breathe in the almost non-existent fragrance of his wife's pillow, was heartbreaking.

When she stood at the opening to the baby's room, it took all her effort to hold back her tears. She wasn't sure how David managed to do the same. Wearing his wife's clothes did not sit right with Birdie, especially with his pain being so raw.

Sure, it had been three years, but time had stood still for his emotions. If he'd moved back to his ranch after their death, things might have been a lot different for him. As it was now, it could have happened mere days ago.

David was there for her when she needed him. Now it was her turn to look out for him. How she would do that, Birdie didn't know, but she was certain an idea would present itself.

She shook herself mentally. David was not looking for a relationship. He wasn't ready to move forward with his life. And likely never would be. Birdie could totally understand it.

Her mind was spinning. She needed to do something. Anything. Keeping busy would stop the unwelcome thoughts. Not only did they confuse her, but they also made Birdie doubt herself.

"It's a shame you don't have chickens," she said suddenly, changing the subject. "They're a good food source."

David stared at her. Was he trying to figure out why she switched subjects so dramatically? It had felt as though they were going down a rabbit hole. One that was upsetting him far more than she liked. Honesty was good, but regrets were not. "We had chickens," he said, his eyes burning into hers. "Garrett rehomed all the animals and critters we had here. I couldn't let them starve to death."

She already knew he had a kind heart. As much as his heart was shattering at that time, he had ensured his animals were well cared for in his absence. It was enough to make her own heart hurt. She reached out and touched his hand again. David glanced down at their entwined hands, and stared. Birdie was certain he would pull his hand away from her. Instead, he placed his other hand over the top of hers effectively trapping her. Not that it bothered her. Not really.

His face softened, and she wondered if that was a good thing. They were stuck here for goodness knew how long, and needed to keep it professional. He would understand that, being a marshal. Except, by his own admission, he was on indefinite leave, so not strictly a marshal.

His eyes opened wide, and Birdie wondered what had happened to cause it. "We should arrange that bath I promised you," he said. "There is no running water, as you've no doubt found out, so you'll need to use the large pot." His eyes closed momentarily, then opened again. "It's what Mae did."

He stood and left the room then, leaving Birdie to her own thoughts. Perhaps it wasn't the best thing for them to be here after all. Despite David insisting, Birdie had her doubts. Staying here with her could make things far worse for him.

~*~

As she lay soaking in the warm water, bubbles up to her neck, Birdie had never appreciated a bath so much as this one.

David found a bottle of his wife's bubble bath, and poured it into the bath. He did that despite Birdie's protests. "It will go to waste otherwise," he said. It was his way of insisting she not feel guilty.

Except she did. Birdie didn't like using anything that belonged to Mae. She felt like an intruder in the dead woman's home. Which, in reality, she was. Despite that, she was thoroughly enjoying the bath. It had been days since she'd been able to bathe – in any shape or form. Her kidnappers had seen to it.

With the water only tepid now, Birdie knew it was time to get out. She reached for a towel, and wrapped herself in it. It was one of the most luxurious towels she'd used for a long time. At least it seemed that way. Less than a week ago, she was snatched, but it felt closer to a month.

She dried herself then reached for the clean clothes she'd laid out to wear. Hygiene was important to Birdie, and she had no intention of donning the same clothes she'd worn since they arrived.

As she stood in the bathroom, near naked, her hair dripping wet, Birdie heard something. What it was, she didn't know, except she was sure it was voices. Men's voices.

Her heart fluttered. Had Lonnie and Hal found her? She dried her hair as quickly as she could. She would not put David in danger to protect her. Birdie glanced about. Nothing in this room screamed weapon. Not that she knew how to use a firearm. Or anything else for that matter. But she would try her best.

Dressing quickly, she glanced in the mirror. She appeared far better now than she did before her bath. She would be eternally grateful for the little things. Living the lifestyle she had until her kidnap, Birdie now realized she'd taken so much for granted.

Birdie and her parents had always endeavored to live below their means. They financially supported several charities they deemed worthy, and along with her mother, Birdie had volunteered her time as well.

It may not have been a lot, but she believed their support made a difference in people's lives.

"Birdie." David's voice came through the door as he knocked gently. "Are you alright?" he asked.

A smile came to her lips. He was worried about her? Did he think she'd drowned? Birdie quietly chuckled. Now decent, she reached over and opened the door.

David stared at her, his eyes grazing her from head to toe. "You look much better," he said. "More relaxed, too."

She rolled her eyes. "Cleaner, do you mean?" They both laughed, and the pair walked down the hallway together. "I thought I heard voices," she said matter-of-factly.

David turned to stare at her. "You did," he said quietly. "We have a visitor." Her heart pounded.

Who was this visitor, and were they safe? As if he could read her mind, David set about reassuring her. "It's a marshal friend. I sent a telegraph early this morning requesting assistance. He's here to help."

Her heart rate slowed, but Birdie was still apprehensive. "He's trustworthy?" she asked quietly. In her heart, she knew David would not put her in imminent danger, but it didn't mean she was as confident about the stranger as he was.

His hand slowly went up around her shoulders. "Do you trust me?" he asked as he stared down into her face.

Birdie's heart pounded. "You know I do. I wouldn't be here with you otherwise."

"Then you know I would not put you in danger." He led her to the sitting room. The stranger was sitting near to the fire. He stood the moment he saw them.

"Birdie, this is Marshal Isaac Asher."

The marshal reached out and took her hand. "Very happy to meet you, I only wish it was under better circumstances." He indicated for Birdie to sit down. "Here's what we know…" he began, then stopped abruptly. "Assuming you want details?" He studied her, then glanced at David.

"I…I think I do," Birdie said cautiously. She wasn't one to shy away from the truth. At least she normally wasn't. In this case, Birdie wasn't sure she wanted to know. She turned to David.

"You don't have to listen if you don't want to. Totally your choice," he said.

As much as Birdie wanted to know, she had dealt with enough bad news lately to last a lifetime. "I'll make coffee," she said firmly as she stood. "How do you take yours Marshal," she asked the newcomer.

He stared at her for long moments before answering. "It's Isaac," he said. "I like my coffee black and strong." He waited until she left the sitting room before speaking again.

Chapter Twelve

David gazed at her as Birdie left the room. He was surprised she'd opted to be kept in the dark. Most of the time she was the exact opposite.

He understood completely why she'd made the decision. She was stressed and afraid. If the news was bad, she may not be able to cope. And according to what Isaac had told him, it was awful.

"Lonnie and Hal," Isaac said.

"Don't know them," David said. "Should I?" He was confused. Isaac said their names as though he should know.

"Elmer Lonigan and Irvin Halstead." The other man said the names firmly. "We've been after them for some time. This is exactly the sort of thing they do – kidnap the heir to a fortune, and hold them for ransom. It seems they underestimated Birdie."

If the situation hadn't been so dire, David probably would have chuckled. Except the circumstances were grim, and lives were at stake. "She sure is a sassy one. Said she'd escaped previously but they found her again."

"Is that so?" Isaac asked. "They wouldn't have liked that. Losing a hostage would make them a laughing stock if word got out."

"How dangerous are they?" David's heart pounded. They were isolated here. It was the reason he'd chosen to bring Birdie here. Except if it meant she was in even more danger, they'd have to leave.

"They are a pair of dangerous fools. I have more men on the way – we'll need the back up. We've been after these two for almost three years. Once they collect the ransom, they kill their victim. Birdie was right to escape. She may not have lasted much longer otherwise."

David turned as he heard her gasp. She stood in the doorway holding a tray with two coffees and a plate of muffins. He hurried over and took the shaking tray from her hands. "Maybe you should sit down," he suggested. Instead, she spun around and left the room.

"Will she be alright?" the marshal asked.

David shrugged. "I hope so. She seems to be fairly resilient," he said, handing a mug of coffee to his friend. He could hear Birdie rattling around in the kitchen – it was her form of stress relief. If the aroma coming from the kitchen was anything to go by, it would be to their advantage.

Shaking himself mentally, David felt overwhelming guilt at his thoughts of moments ago. Birdie was a wonderful person who did not do anything to cause what happened to her. People like Lonnie and Hal, as they called themselves, believed they had the right to take whatever or whomever they wished.

As a marshal, and a man of high morals, David believed it was up to him to stop criminals like those two. He would do everything in his power to put an end to their reign of terror.

He continued to hear Birdie moving around the kitchen. Until he didn't. David's heart pounded with fear. How could anyone have entered the house without his knowledge? There were two marshals here for goodness sake.

He was on his feet in seconds, Isaac close behind. The kitchen was devoid of activity, but something sure did smell good. David ran into the pantry. No sign of Birdie there either. His heart felt like it was pushing out of his chest. He would not lose her on his watch.

His mind was whirling with possibilities. There hadn't been any doors opened or closed. He would have heard them. The only option left to him was to search the house, room by room. It would be just like Birdie to find something to keep her mind occupied. If she couldn't find something to do, she would surely invent a chore that needed doing.

It didn't take long until they found her in the main bedroom. The pile of sheets on the floor told him she'd stripped the sheets from the bed and replaced them with a fresh set. Now she sat on the side of the bed, holding a pillow close to her, breathing in the essence of his wife.

Tears rolled down her cheeks. He didn't have to be a genius to work out why. "It's alright, Birdie," he said, sitting down next to her. "Her scent is almost diminished. As much as I would like to keep it forever, it's not possible." David gently took the pillow from her hands. He breathed in the last remnants of Mae before pulling the covering off the pillow. As much as his heart was breaking, he was far more concerned about Birdie. Nothing he did would bring his wife and child back, but he would do everything possible to keep Birdie safe and out of the hands of killers.

Birdie had been subdued for the rest of the day. Even at supper she barely spoke. The two men sat at the table while she washed the dishes. She'd rejected their offer of help several times. In the end, they gave up.

David stoked the woodstove and refueled it. If they wanted coffee in the morning, it was crucial to keep it burning. The men talked in low voices, hoping

Birdie couldn't hear. There was no plan in place, something that bothered David immensely.

"We will be joined by more marshals tomorrow," Isaac said. "At least two, maybe more." He studied David who said nothing, then shrugged. "You know how it is."

He did know. David had spent more than twenty years as a marshal. One day after his twenty-first birthday, he'd applied to join the ranks of the elite lawmen. His father, a sheriff at the time, supported David in his endeavor. He wanted to make his father proud, and was certain he'd done that.

He'd met Mae during an assignment. David should have known better – lawmen marrying never worked out. They were away more often than they were home. It put a huge strain on their marriage. It didn't seem to bother Mae. At least that's what she told him. Leaving her out here alone, on their isolated ranch wasn't something he was proud of, and eventually it got the better of him. When she was heavy with their child, he applied for leave. As it turned out, it was the best thing he could have done. Spending those last weeks with his wife were now precious memories.

David knew he needed to go back to doing what he did best, but the pull was no longer there. Besides, his time was better spent protecting Birdie right now.

He would not abandon Birdie in her time of need. What sort of person would that make him?

The answer was clear – a man who couldn't live with himself.

Chapter Thirteen

Birdie had not thought about what she was doing. It was a natural thing to do – change the sheets. If David hadn't been out here for some time, everything would be dusty. So far, that had proven to be true.

She'd dusted the robe and the cupboards in the main bedroom, then tackled the sheets. Mae had everything carefully stored, which made it easy for Birdie to find what she needed.

When it came time to pull the sheets off the bed, she did that easily and without concern. The moment Mae's pillow was in her hands, she accidentally inhaled the faded scent of David's dead wife, and emotion had overcome her.

Her heart pounded at the thought of not only what Mae had endured, but also of David's devastation at his family's demise. Knowing David, even for such a short time, Birdie was certain the former marshal would have blamed himself.

Was it the reason he left and never returned? She could only imagine the pain he felt at returning to a place where his entire life had come to a standstill. Where death surrounded him at every turn.

Holding Mae's pillow close to her heart, Birdie couldn't bring herself to remove the pillow case that was slightly infused with the essence of Mae. It made no sense to turn a pillow into a monument, but she felt in her heart, it's what she needed to do.

For David's sake.

Tears rolled down her face unbidden. This was not what she'd planned. She would change the bed, and get out of the room. As quickly as possible, then tackle another room. Although Birdie knew she couldn't bring herself to go into the baby's room.

It would be another kind of heartache to do so.

She could still see the pain on David's face as he stood in the doorway earlier. Glancing at the furniture and the tiny clothes. Her own heart had skipped a beat when she saw them, and she was a complete stranger to this family.

He was a broken man. And yet, he didn't hesitate to help her when she needed him.

She'd barely noticed him entering the room, but his concern seemed to be more with her than his own feelings. David's arm crept up around her shoulders, as he tried to comfort her. Then he'd taken the pillow from her. She averted her eyes as he'd breathed in those last remaining remnants of his wife. The pain she'd previously witnessed earlier seemed to have diminished, and yet, she still knew his heart was shattered. It would be for a very long time, Birdie was certain.

They sat in silence on the edge of the bed. It seemed like they'd been there for hours, but Birdie knew it was only a matter of minutes. She had supper to arrange, and needed to check on the food she had cooking. There was little else for her to do, so cooking and cleaning was thankfully, filling in her time.

There was little option – she couldn't go outside, so was stuck in here. At least she would be kept busy. With other marshals expected soon, she'd better check over the food supplies and work out what she would feed the men. They would no doubt be hungry, most men were, and that would keep her busy.

Where they would all sleep was another question. She hadn't ventured into the other rooms. The doors had been closed, and Birdie felt it wasn't her place to pry. David and Mae had no doubt planned for a large family. Although she wasn't certain they'd built the ranch house. Still, a big family, especially of boys, was always welcomed on a ranch. At least it's what she had heard. Being brought up in the city, she wasn't privy to the thoughts of country folk.

Movement next to her told Birdie the pillow case had been pulled from the place it lay for the past three years. David threw it across the room to sit atop the sheets she'd placed there earlier. Putting the pillow aside, he pulled her into his arms. It took all Birdie's strength not to melt into his arms and let her heartache overtake her.

It would have been so easy to do. David had proven himself to be caring and protective, but the truth of the matter was, he needed her as much as she needed him.

"Marshals are used to sleeping rough," Isaac said, responding to Birdie's question about sleeping arrangements. "And we sure aren't used to this sort of food. You're an excellent cook," he added.

Birdie shrugged. It was meant as a compliment, but her cooking was nothing like he'd made out. "My skills in the kitchen are not that good. I can make basic meals, and bake a few things like muffins and pound cake. I have made the occasional apple pie, too," she said. That was her cue to take the pie out of the oven. "Speaking of which," she said, placing it on the counter top. "It needs to cool for a few minutes, then I can serve it up."

"David, my boy," Isaac said, laughter in his voice, "you've been keeping secrets from me." Both men laughed, and Birdie couldn't help but join in. It was nice to have her cooking complimented, but she was convinced it was nothing special.

Staring out the kitchen window momentarily while she waited to cut the apple pie, Birdie saw movement. "There's someone out there," she said, her voice shaking. "At least I think there is." It was almost dusk, making it difficult to know for certain.

David was next to her in seconds. "Get down," he said urgently, and pulled her to the floor. Isaac stood and was out of the kitchen within moments. Birdie heard the front door close behind him.

David hovered over Birdie, protecting her from potentially flying bullets.

It felt like a lifetime until Isaac returned. "If someone was there, they've gone," he said. "It could have been one of the wild creatures that frequent the area." He sat back at the table, and waited for his pie.

If it hadn't been so serious, Birdie knew she would laugh. She managed to keep her amusement to herself, and dished each of the men a large slice of pie. Along with the pie, the bowl of clotted cream soon disappeared. Once their bowls were empty, they were quickly refilled.

Birdie wasn't used to big eaters like these two. Her father was, of course, much older, and didn't eat anywhere near as much. Still, she didn't mind. They were her protectors, and she owed them her life. And as much pie as they could eat.

After supper, the pair disappeared into the sitting room, leaving Birdie to clean up. She preferred it that way. Hearing about the crimes of Lonnie and Hal did not appease her anxiety. It only proved to make it worse.

At the back of her mind the entire time was the sleeping arrangements. Not knowing what sat behind the two closed doors worried Birdie. Were there beds in those rooms? If there weren't, was she expected to sleep with David? He had no sofa, only individual chairs, so it wasn't ideal.

And what of the marshals? Where would they sleep? Isaac said they were used to sleeping rough, but it didn't sit well with Birdie. Perhaps she could do some digging and check if there were enough spare blankets to make up some pallets for the marshals.

Even as she thought about it, Birdie knew there was a slim chance of finding enough blankets to accommodate even two more marshals when they arrived.

Chapter Fourteen

David would be relieved when back up arrived. With only himself and Isaac, it meant Isaac had to leave the house alone. That wasn't the way marshals worked. They always had a partner to back them up should it be required.

Only he couldn't and wouldn't leave Birdie in the house by herself. From what he'd heard about her abductors, they wouldn't hesitate to lure her protectors away, and snatch her up yet again. Being the sole heir to the Valence fortune, Birdie was worth a lot to them. He had no doubt Douglas Valence would pay whatever they demanded.

And therein was the problem. Once the ransom was paid, Birdie was no longer of any use to them. In fact, she would be a burden. According to Isaac, the pair killed their victims the moment their demands were met.

It was then it hit him. Had her father already paid the ransom and now they needed to eliminate all loose ends? Meaning Birdie?

He shook his head mentally. How did anyone act in this way? The best outcome would be to capture those monsters and lock them away for life. Better still, hang them by the neck until they were dead. A dead criminal was always the best kind in David's view.

He couldn't imagine any judge allowing serial killers like these two to live. Still, he wasn't a judge, and it wasn't his job to make those decisions. His job was to find them and ensure they went before the court for a proper punishment.

"Would anyone like more coffee? I'm going to bed if that's alright?" As if on cue, she yawned. David should have known she'd be tired. It had been a big day, not only with the travel, but stress was exhausting, and Birdie had been quite anxious as well.

"Better not," he said, getting to his feet. "I'll never sleep tonight."

"I would appreciate it," Isaac said. "I'm on first watch. I can get it myself, though," he said, then headed into the kitchen with his empty mug.

Birdie headed toward the bedroom, but stopped suddenly. She was only a few steps away from the main bedroom. "Which room has a single bed?" she asked.

David stared at her. Hadn't she checked the other rooms? They were completely empty. "You'll need to sleep with me." He put a hand up in front of himself to stop her protests. "It's the only bed apart from the crib." Birdie simply stared. It was as though she didn't comprehend what he was saying. Only he was certain she did. "I promise, I will keep my distance," he said.

Until the moment Birdie came on the scene, he'd considered selling the ranch. It had stood empty all this time, simply collecting dust. Garrett had him convinced he either had to sell it, or move back in. David didn't want to do either. His heart shattered all over again merely thinking about it.

For the moment, it was all on hold. Once the kidnappers were caught and behind bars, he would dedicate some time to working out the benefits of each scenario. At least then his brother might get off his back. Then again, depending on his decision, he may not.

He wanted David to move back to the ranch and sort himself out, and get on with his life. Garrett had told him time and again, David needed to marry and move back into the ranch.

Except he'd already endured enough heartache to last a lifetime. He wasn't ready to go through it all over again. No, it was better to stay single, than lose his heart to someone he might eventually lose.

Birdie spun around to face him. She stared into his eyes, not moving her gaze for what seemed to be never-ending. He knew, however, it was an incredibly short time. Finally, she pulled her gaze from his face.

"I really have no choice, do I?" she asked, her pale face filling with pink blushes. David didn't like it any more than Birdie did, but their options were limited due to the lack of furniture.

The plan had always been to fill each of the rooms with beds, side tables and more. That way Mae's parents could come and visit after the baby was born. After his wife and son's deaths, all and any plans he had were put on hold.

Except David didn't expect to wait this long to return home. He had never planned for the tragedy that resulted, and until Birdie arrived on the scene, was adamant he would never return. His plans were derailed the second Birdie entered the dance, and their eyes met across the room.

He could pick out a terrified woman, even at that distance. David really had no choice but to ensure her safety.

The one thing he regretted about that night, was kissing her. His lips had tingled for far longer than was acceptable.

It was something he would not forget for a very long time.

"Not if you want to sleep tonight," he told her. "You should find nightgowns in the drawers, and a thick robe will be there as well, I believe. If not, it will be somewhere in that room."

She nodded but didn't answer. Instead, Birdie turned and headed toward the bedroom once again. "Oh," she said, suddenly facing him again. "I'd intended looking for blankets to make up some pallets for the marshals."

"They won't be here until tomorrow," David said, his eyes watching her every move. "Isaac won't need it tonight – he's on first watch. I'll take over at first light."

It seemed to appease her, and Birdie headed into the bedroom. He heard her rifling through the drawers, no doubt looking for a nightgown. Minutes later she flew out of the door and hurried to the bathroom, nightgown and robe over her arm.

He knew Birdie was reluctant to use any of Mae's clothes or toiletries, but she had nothing of her own. There was simply no choice. David understood the most difficult thing about this scenario of Birdie wearing Mae's clothes, was she would likely smell like his wife.

The worst thing he could do, would be to fall for this woman. And all because she was wearing his wife's clothes, and using her perfume and soap.

He stared after her as Birdie made her way down the passageway into the bathroom. She closed the door, and he heard the click of the lock. Mae had never locked the door, not even when they'd had a disagreement.

Still, Birdie was not Mae. She was in a house with two men she didn't know, being pursued by two other men who wanted her dead.

It was little wonder she was locking doors and not wanting to sleep in the same bed as one of the strangers charged with protecting her. Tomorrow would be even worse for Birdie. At least two more marshals were coming to help out.

One way or the other, between them, they would apprehend Lonnie and Hal. If it was the last thing he ever did, David would ensure they would never get near Birdie again.

Chapter Fifteen

Birdie closed the bathroom door and locked it. She quickly undressed, then held the nightgown David's wife had worn. Had she spent her last hours in this garment? The thought had her heart breaking all over again.

She brought the gown to her face and breathed in. It held the faintest odor, but it wasn't the same as the pillow. This smelled more like cleaning solutions, which made sense. David would have ensured everything was thoroughly cleaned, Birdie was certain. Pulling the nightgown over her head, she still was riddled with guilt.

It was bad enough having to wear Mae's gowns. Not to mention her shoes and undergarments. Now she was taking something far more personal. As she pulled the nightgown down around her knees, Birdie had another thought. Had Mae died in this gown? It had her gasping. She wanted to rip the garment into pieces. Shred it into tiny bits. That way she never had to wear it again.

Almost the moment the upsetting thought came to her, she dismissed it. She felt certain David would not have keep such an item. Birdie ran her hands down the cotton nightgown. It was so soft to touch, and it felt like she'd worn it many times over.

There was little deviation with this garment, from those she wore back home. Now she wondered about her father. She could only imagine how desperate he must be for news of her safety. She made a mental note to talk to David about it. Perhaps he could get word to her father, letting him know she was alive and well.

"Are you okay?" David's voice came through the door as he lightly tapped it. "Do you need help?" he asked. Birdie could tell from his voice he was teasing, so she let it go.

"I'll be out momentarily," she called through the door, keeping her voice as sweet as she could, given the circumstances.

Birdie glanced at her reflection. Her hair was a mess and she had black circles under her eyes. Not surprising, she decided. She pulled the pins from her hair, and released the plait which was previously pinned to her head. Running her fingers through her hair, she was able to release her long locks, but not eliminate the tangles.

Opening a cupboard door, she looked for a brush. Birdie knew it would be yet another of Mae's belongings, but she had little choice. Besides, she didn't think Mae would mind, had she known.

She brushed as quickly as possible, knowing she wouldn't attempt one hundred strokes tonight. It wasn't late, but Birdie was exhausted and could barely stand. Glancing in the mirror again, she noticed how pale her skin was. To fix it and cover up her current state of health, Birdie slapped at both cheeks until a semblance of color came back into them.

She replaced the brush, adding her own hair supplies to the cupboard. Now she was ready to leave the room.

Unlocking the door, she pulled it open, only to find David standing so close he almost tumbled inside. "There you are," he said, his gaze going from her head to her toes. His eyes seemed pinned to the floor.

Birdie glanced down, and that's when she saw it. Or should she say them? Her bare feet were showing beneath the robe she wore. It made her wonder if David was transfixed by her state of undress, or was he reminiscing about his wife's belongings? She would probably never know.

"Isaac is set up in the sitting room," he said. "I'm going to bed shortly." He stared into her face for an unsettling amount of time. "You look beat. Come on, I'll walk you to the bedroom."

He was right, she was beat. If her head didn't hit the pillow soon, Birdie was sure she would collapse from lack of sleep. As they walked side-by-side down the corridor, it would have been so easy to lean against him and close her eyes.

Birdie knew she shouldn't but she felt comfortable around David. Isaac too. They had a comradery like she'd never seen before. Isaac was more than a marshal. He was David's friend, Birdie was certain of it. It made her wonder if they'd worked together in the past.

No matter. She was far too tired to think about insignificant details. She just needed to get into the bedroom, lay down on the bed, and get some much needed sleep.

It felt like she was floating on air, but Birdie didn't care. She was exhausted to the point she couldn't even open her eyes. The peacefulness of her surroundings lulled her into a deep sleep. The covers were up around her shoulders, but she couldn't remember getting into bed, let alone pulling the covers up.

Instead of questioning everything, Birdie closed her eyes and let her mind drift. She would think about her life back in Helena, and how much she loved her father.

There was movement nearby, but she couldn't find the energy to open her eyes to work out what it was. Moments later, the bed sagged. The deep sleep she found herself in stopped Birdie from investigating what was happening. She'd done so much in the past twelve hours or so, and simply couldn't function without enough sleep.

She rolled over and let herself drift into oblivion. It was such a nice place to be.

Chapter Sixteen

One minute they were moving down the hallway toward the bedroom, and the next Birdie had gone limp as she huddled into him.

She was exhausted, there was no doubt about it. Not only had she travelled to the ranch from town under the guise of being a prisoner, but she'd worked her pretty butt off for the remainder of the day.

He wasn't stupid enough to think it was the travel alone. Stress and anxiety had played a huge role in her tiredness. As he lifted her into his arms and tucked her up in bed, Birdie barely moved. Pulling the covers up over her seemed somehow…personal.

He missed the days when he would do the same for Mae. David loved Mae dearly, but it was now clear he had to move on. Her memory would never evaporate, but he must concentrate on Birdie and keep her safe.

Tomorrow was another day entirely. He hoped she slept soundly for as long as she needed. He silently pulled the window coverings closed – that should help her sleep a little longer. Now it was time for him to turn in. Isaac was relying on him to take over at dawn. David would be more than a little grateful when the other marshals arrived.

He gently lay down on top of the bed, ensuring he didn't wake Birdie. Under the covers would definitely be warmer, but David needed to be prepared for anything. Besides, the fire was burning nicely – before Birdie even announced she was going to bed, he'd seen to the bedroom fire. It could get quite cold in there this time of the year.

It seemed as though his head had no sooner hit the pillow, than he heard movement. David listened carefully. His hope was Isaac was helping himself to more coffee. He lay back down again.

A click and he was convinced the door had been opened. As quietly as he could, David pushed himself off the bed, reaching for the gun he had placed under his pillow. Silently but cautiously, he moved toward the sitting room.

His relief was palpable when he was confronted by three additional men standing in the room, along with Isaac. All three marshals were known to him, which was David's preference. It meant he knew the way they worked. It also confirmed they would be willing to exert themselves a little more to round up the killers.

As he let down his guard and strolled into the sitting room, four men with guns all spun around to face him. At least he knew they were on alert. "David," Isaac said, his voice barely above a whisper. "We have visitors. I think you all know each other," he added.

David shook the hand of each marshal. It had been a long time, but still, time doesn't erase all memories, as he knew first hand. "Welcome, and thank you," he told them. "Let me arrange refreshments. I'm sure you've been travelling for hours." He didn't wait for a response, but headed into the kitchen.

David knew once he'd fed the men, he could go back to bed and get a good night's sleep. Having four marshals here made things far better. They could work in shifts of two on guard, two sleeping. It also meant he didn't have to worry. He could provide Birdie with around the clock protection of his own. Leaving the marshals to find Lonnie and Hal.

Still, it didn't mean he was letting his guard down. He was here to protect her – he'd promised Birdie from the moment she'd come to him, he would defend her. And it was exactly what he intended to do.

Trying to keep the noise to a minimum, he set the food and drinks on the kitchen table, then refilled the coffee pot. David knew it would be depleted by morning otherwise. Thankfully, Birdie had baked muffins earlier in the day, so he had something to give the men. They would no doubt be hungry after their long trip.

He strolled into the sitting room, expecting to find them all sitting around, talking between themselves. Except they were still in the huddle he'd found them in earlier. It told David there was something they weren't telling him. "What's going on?" he asked, his voice barely above a whisper. It was better he knew, otherwise it could put Birdie's life in danger.

Not one of the marshal's answered. His gaze went from one man to the other. Still no one answered. "We should move into the kitchen," he finally said. "I have coffee and muffins waiting there." David was feeling annoyed, but knew he shouldn't. They were just doing their job. He was not a marshal, not while he was still on indefinite leave, but David wasn't certain he'd ever go back to the job he'd once loved so much.

He put a finger to his lips, trying to keep the noise down. Without meaning to, four men planning strategies, often got out of hand.

Once everyone was seated, David again moved his gaze from one man to the next. Finally, Isaac spoke. "There have been sightings of Lonnie and Hal. Not here, but in town. They are searching Langley, trying to find Birdie."

"They must have still been in town when we transported her here." To say he was disappointed they'd not been put off the trail was an understatement. It was then he realized the implications. "We need more men," David said firmly. "The citizens of Langley need protecting also."

"Already done," Isaac said. "There are four more marshals in town. We are determined to catch those murderous kidnappers this time."

David's heart pounded. He was fully aware the four marshals stationed here were capable of protecting Birdie, but he needed a plan as well. What if Lonnie and Hal brought reinforcements and God forbid, the marshals were all killed or injured? He needed a way to get Birdie to safety.

In the back of his mind, something was brewing. He couldn't think what it was, but there was a niggle in his mind. What had he had been told about this place long ago? Of course he should know what it was. This was his home, although he would be the first to admit he hadn't spent as much time here as he would have liked. He especially would have spent more time with Mae. Had he known he would lose her so soon, he assuredly would have.

David shook himself mentally. What's past is past, and there was no way to change it. Shaping the future is what he needed to do now.

Chapter Seventeen

Birdie awoke from a deep sleep.

Darkness still surrounded her, but she sensed it wasn't still night. Turning in the bed, Birdie found she was alone. She'd awoken during the night to find David laying on top of the bed, fully dressed. He was a decent man, she knew it from the moment their eyes met across the dance hall that night.

He'd proven it time and again ever since.

Low chatter came from another room. Most likely the kitchen. She should get herself dressed and make breakfast – David and Isaac would be hungry. Birdie had no doubt about it. She pulled back the dark covering from the window.

Glancing outside it was clear time had gotten away from her. It was well past dawn, her preferred time to rise. There was so much to be done, and so little time to do it. Birdie knew her mind was trying to keep her from worrying, and she wasn't complaining.

Snatching up her clothes, she carefully opened the bedroom door, peeking around the corner to ensure neither of the men were around. Confirming it was clear, she hurried to the bathroom, clothes in hand. Locking the door behind her, Birdie saw to her ablutions, then quickly dressed. She left her hair until last, putting off using Mae's brush.

Instead of brooding over it every time she needed to fix her hair, Birdie decided she would plan for the day she had her own belongings once more. Otherwise, she would be heartbroken each and every time she had to ensure she looked presentable.

She stood with her hand on the door handle, finding the courage to leave the bathroom. She'd seen the looks David gave her when she wore his wife's clothes. Having her here was painful for him. From the little she knew, he'd spent the past three years trying to forget the pain of her death, and that of his newborn son.

Wearing Mae's clothes was not helping him to heal, and was surely doing the opposite. Regardless, she had no choice. Unless she wanted to dress in the men's clothes she wore to get here.

Birdie shook herself mentally. She would never be convinced to do that again. She wasn't sure how men put up with clothes that made them feel closed in.

The very thought made her shiver.

She quickly opened the door and headed down the hallway, returning to the bedroom. Carefully folding the nightgown she'd worn, Birdie glanced at the bed. There was no way she would leave this room until the bed was made. It wasn't too bad, she'd slept like the dead. With David laying on top of the covers, the other side of the bed wasn't very messed up at all.

Glancing around the room, she ensured all was in order. There was nothing worse than an untidy bedroom and an unmade bed. Mother had drilled it into her since Birdie was a small child.

Thinking about her mother made Birdie sad. She'd been gone so long and was dearly missed. What Father was thinking now was worrying her. Did he know she was still alive? She hated to think he'd paid a large ransom and hadn't been rewarded with her return.

There was no doubt in Birdie's mind he would have paid the ransom post haste.

This wouldn't do, she finally told herself. Standing around woolgathering wasn't getting anything done. Instead, she headed to the kitchen.

It was there she was confronted by two complete strangers.

Neither man seemed threatening, and they each held a mug of coffee. Heart pounding, Birdie glanced around the room. In the corner, next to the stove, was David, pouring coffee. Relief filled her.

One of the men at the table stood, and extended his hand. "Good morning, Miss Valence," he told her. "I am Marshal Jess Charles. This here is Marshal Tucker Roberts."

The other man glanced up, then stood. "Miss Valence," he said, nodding his head. "Nice to meet you. Er, except for the circumstances," he hurriedly added.

"Please call me Birdie," she said, then strolled across the kitchen to join David at the stove. "I'd better organise breakfast," she said, not acknowledging these two strangers had alarmed her.

David laughed. "We all had breakfast hours ago. It's mid-morning." He grinned and she was devastated. "You were exhausted, so I let you sleep." Without warning, he put his arms around her. "There is nothing you need to do except rest. We are all capable of looking after ourselves."

Birdie doubted it, but didn't voice her opinion. "Two more for lunch, then?" she asked.

"Three," David said. "Isaac and Douglas are sleeping. They'll likely rise for lunch." He reached for another mug. "Tea or coffee?" he asked.

"Tea," she said, still feeling somewhat alarmed. This was a whole new scenario for her. These men all seemed at home, and appeared to have no concerns in the world. It was the complete opposite of how Birdie felt. "Thank you," she added. Forgetting her manners was unforgiveable.

"Take a seat," David told her. "What would you like for breakfast?"

"I…" She couldn't let him look after her in this way. It was her job, not his. Birdie shook her head, feeling bewildered about the entire situation she was now faced with.

"I'm afraid the muffins are all gone. We got hungry last night." Her first reaction was one of annoyance. Then he grinned and Birdie knew she couldn't be mad at him. His smile was contagious, and it made her laugh. Goodness knows she needed it. There wasn't a lot to laugh about lately, and it felt good.

David placed the mug in front of her.

She glanced up at him and smiled. As much as Birdie knew she shouldn't, she really liked him. Not because he was protecting her, and ensuring her safety. But because he was a decent and kind man. Never before had she felt this way about another man.

Most of the men who wanted to court her, only wanted her money. David didn't even know of her father's fortune when he met her. Even now when he did know, he treated her as an equal. Would-be suitors treated her like the heiress she was. Granted, it's what she was, but knowing the only reason they wanted to marry her was because of her father's money, grated.

Still, she knew David was not interested in her in that way. Nor did she have feelings for him. They were thrown together under difficult circumstances, and when it was all over, they would each go their own way.

Chapter Eighteen

The moment David put his arms around Birdie he regretted it. They were not in a relationship of any sort, and definitely not married. It meant he had no right to touch her in anyway.

Except Birdie hadn't complained. Not one iota.

When she first entered the kitchen, she seemed shell-shocked. The sight of two strangers likely frightened her. He should have planned for when she awoke, but hadn't thought about it. He mentally chastised himself. David knew he had to do better. Just because Birdie was well educated did not mean she would not be scared by strange men in the house.

"What am I getting you to eat?" David asked again. It was easy to see he would need to force the issue. Instead of answering, she shook her head. David knew he couldn't let it go. Birdie needed to keep her strength up.

He hoped it wouldn't come to this, but they may need to flee the house.

Slicing bread ready to toast, he studied her. It was clear Birdie was embarrassed. About what, he wasn't certain. Surely it wasn't because she'd slept in? David had noticed she preferred to be busy, but she needed to rest. If they did need to run, she would need all her energy.

With the toast ready, he presented it to her, along with butter, jam, and honey. She could take her pick.

Instead of being delighted, Birdie glanced down at it in horror. "I…" David could see she was upset, but couldn't fathom why. "I should be looking after you, not the other way around," she finally said. Except it wasn't true.

He sat down next to her, putting an arm around her shoulders. "All marshals know how to cook. Of course, we appreciate it when you do your magic in the kitchen," he said, then winked, "but it doesn't mean you are tied to the stove. Now eat up," he added. His last words came out as demanding, which wasn't his intention.

Normally, David would leave Birdie to her own devices. Except he wasn't certain she would actually eat if he wasn't there next to her. Sipping his coffee, he stayed put, not saying another word.

She silently ate, which pleased him. After yesterday's mammoth effort, she needed sustenance. Today would be different – he would make sure of it. If Birdie fell in a heap from exhaustion yet again, David knew he would never be able to forgive himself.

Oh, he knew the reasoning behind it all. He'd done the same thing himself. Keep busy and you will forget all your troubles and woes. Except David knew from first hand experience, it wasn't the case.

Instead of forgetting, and sending the hurt to the back of your mind, you moved it a little closer to the front. The pain was always there, and never went away. Letting yourself mourn what used to be turned out to be the best way.

He glanced down at Birdie's plate. Thankfully, she'd eaten everything put in front of her, and was now sipping her tea. When he glanced up, Jess and Tucker, the two marshals sitting opposite them, were studying him. What they thought of his tactics, David didn't know. And frankly, he didn't care either.

Someone had to look after Birdie's well-being, and if it turned out to be him, David was not complaining.

"May I go now?" she asked quietly. "I've been a good girl and eaten my food." She smiled on the last part, and David grinned. Even through adversity, she managed to make a joke. The more he got to know Birdie, the more he liked her.

He needed to be careful – she was already getting under his skin. And they'd only known each other for a matter of days.

Almost the moment Birdie stood, he noticed the transformation. She went from demure, cooperating Birdie, to a woman with a mission. First, she loaded up the woodstove to ensure it was burning evenly, and while the fire became more even, she washed the dishes.

After that, she hurried into the pantry and collected a number of ingredients. It wasn't long before she'd added all those ingredients to a bowl. The end result, according to Birdie, was a pound cake. It wasn't even in the oven yet, and still David found himself anticipating when it could be eaten.

He hadn't realized how much he'd missed home cooked meals. The diner was good, but their meals did not compare to what Birdie had been making. David was reluctant to return to the ranch, even on a temporary basis, but knew he needed to do so for Birdie's benefit.

Now he was back here and gotten over the initial flashbacks and heartbreak, he was beginning to feel at home again. He'd been gone for so long, he hadn't even appreciated how much he missed being here.

It was a place he'd loved from the day he saw it. His vision was to run this ranch the way it was meant to be. Except he was still a marshal, and his job took priority. It's funny how things change. Three years ago he'd lost everything he loved. His wife, his son, and his home. The latter being his own fault.

He'd put his job on hold until he was ready to work as a marshal again. At least that's what he told himself.

Now, David knew he would never go back to his life as a marshal. He wasn't sure how or why he'd come to that conclusion, but the thought came to him unbidden. Was it because of Birdie? Because with her he'd found some semblance of peace? He wasn't sure what it was about her, but he felt a glimmer of hope when he was around her.

Not in a romantic way. It definitely wasn't like that. There was no way he was falling in love with Birdie. Nor would she feel this way about him.

No, it was something else. Her positivity perhaps? David shook himself mentally. This line of thought was getting him nowhere. He stood, stretching himself out, after having sat at the table for far too long. "What can I do to help?" he asked. Doing nothing was not the way he worked. He fully understood why Birdie needed to keep busy, because he was the same.

Although, in his case, David was able to sit for short bursts and just be. Let his mind relax for a while before taking on the next task. Whether it was a nervous reaction, he wasn't certain, but Birdie seemed to go from one task to another without a break in between.

Did it mean she would fall in a heap again tonight? He would try his best to get her to slow down.

Chapter Nineteen

Birdie knew David was simply looking out for her, and she was grateful. She really was. It was difficult for her to even think about eating when she had so much to do. Now the cake was in the oven, she could concentrate on lunch. If only they had chickens, she could…

They? Where did that come from?

She shook herself mentally. For now, there were plenty of supplies in the pantry. The three marshals had brought a box of supplies with them, which Birdie found to be thoughtful, and definitely appreciated. They'd brought eggs, flour, sugar, vegetables, and beef. They even bought two chickens, ready to be cooked. The icebox already had milk, butter, and cream, and they'd bought more. Birdie was grateful for the additional supplies and would put them to good use.

She spun around to face David. "Did you say there was a root cellar?" Moments after the words were out, she wanted to take them back. Three years had passed since anyone had been here. Whatever happened to still be in the root cellar would be beyond redemption. "Forget it. Nothing down there will be editable."

David shrugged. He had to know she was right. But it was still a good idea to check it out. Except she couldn't force him to do it.

"I'll take a look," he said nonchalantly. She didn't blame him – if it was as bad as she expected it would be, David could find himself retching at the smell.

Regardless of what he found, Birdie still had to prepare something for lunch. She had five hungry men to feed. She stood staring out of the window as she mentally went through her options. There was a variety of vegetables as well as several large pieces of beef. She could either make a stew or a beef pie, served with vegetables.

She sighed. Birdie had slept far too late for stew, so a pie it was. She placed the frying pan on the stove, and left it to warm up while she headed to the pantry once again. She hadn't cooked for this many people before, so had to calculate how many servings she would get from a piece of beef. Birdie mostly cooked after her mother died, but brought in a chef for special occasions, such as dinner parties. Thankfully, they were few and far between. Large numbers of guests was not particularly comfortable for her.

When she returned to the kitchen, David was missing. "He's gone to check out the root cellar,"

Jess offered. "I imagine it won't be good." He raised his eyebrows as if in question.

Birdie grimaced. "I suppose you are right," she said, but knew it had to be done. Instead of dwelling on what might or may not be found in the root cellar, she set to work preparing the pie. After chopping an onion and frying it in the pan, she sliced the meat into similar sized cubes. Browning the meat gave off a delicious aroma, and Birdie knew it would only get better.

While the meat and onions sizzled in the pan, she worked on the pastry. This was the slowest part of the process. All that rolling, folding, and repeating it all several times over. Birdie was grateful to their former cook, Bella.

The older Italian lady had taught Birdie a lot. Thanks to her, Birdie enjoyed cooking, especially baking sweet treats, such as muffins and cakes. It was a sad day when Bella retired to spend more time with her family.

She turned back to the frying pan, and stirred the contents again. It was almost time for the combination to go in the pastry base. Birdie opened the oven door. It was good and hot, just like she needed it to be.

Closing the door again, she greased the pie dish, and added pastry to the base. Giving the meat mixture a last stir, she placed it over the pastry, then added the top sheet of pastry, brushing it with egg to help it brown. This then went in the oven.

There was still plenty of pastry left over for another pie, but she wouldn't serve two pies for lunch. Instead, she planned on apple pie for dessert with supper tonight. No matter what she served up, she knew these men would eat it. If she was truthful, it was nice cooking for people who appreciated it. Father was much older now, and only picked at his food.

The thought made her wonder yet again, how he was coping with the situation. If only there was some way to let him know she was alive and well.

Birdie glanced at the men as they sat around the table.

"This food is excellent," Douglas said. "Best I've had for a long time."

These men didn't get home cooked meals often, so Birdie didn't take his words to mean much. Before she had a chance to respond, the others all chimed in, too.

"Best I've had," Jess said.

Then it was Tucker who spoke. "I certainly can't complain," he said as he finished off his apple pie.

Isaac sat grinning. "Birdie already knows how I feel. If this big oaf," pointing to David, "doesn't marry her, I might have to claim Birdie for myself."

How did the conversation get to this? Birdie was floored.

"Hey!" David almost shouted. "What's this about marriage?" It seemed he finally realized Isaac was joking, as he then grinned. "I'd marry her in a heartbeat if it meant you couldn't," he said with a grin.

Birdie had heard enough. She picked up her empty bowl, and went to the sink. In doing so, she glanced out of the window. Turning back to face the men at the table, she considered whether she should tell them. Last time it was a wild animal. Would it be the same this time?

"Birdie?" David asked. "What is going on in your pretty little head?"

She focused her gaze on him. "Probably nothing." Moments later he was by her side. Soon all five men were checking whatever was in the distance.

Could this be the moment of truth?

Chapter Twenty

David promised himself to clear the root cellar earlier this morning. He had been down there and boy, did it stink. There was no way he'd let Birdie down there until he'd cleaned it out, and somehow got rid of the smell.

While he checked it all out, he remembered what he'd been trying to recall about the ranch. At least he thought he did. It could be a game changer, but he would have to investigate further before saying anything. Although he did mention it to Isaac, but the details were sketchy.

As they all stood staring out the kitchen window, David truly wished he had checked the root cellar out more thoroughly while he was in a position to do so. The stench of rotting food had him retreating far quicker than he'd anticipated. Next time he ventured down the ladder, he would have a bandana over his nose and mouth. It wouldn't completely quell the awful odor, but would certainly help.

Tomorrow he would go back with a large box, and dispose of the rotting supplies he'd found. That meant everything had to go. He planned to light a fire in the old metal barrel, and destroy everything he removed. In his mind, it was beyond the point of saving any of it for compost. It wasn't like the vegetable garden was viable, not after three years of neglect. Still, he could be surprised.

He resisted the urge to shake his head. If he did that, David knew Birdie would want to know what he was thinking.

Isaac suddenly pulled the window coverings partially closed. "Kill the lantern," he ordered, and Jess obliged.

"You see something?" David wanted to know. Before he'd even finished the sentence, Jess and Tucker had their guns out of their holsters. They were ready for action.

Isaac's hand went up to stall them. David knew the drill – marshals were meant to be cautious, and didn't pounce until they were certain. "I'm not sure. Let's study the area a little longer."

Jess and Tucker held tight to their guns. They weren't taking any chances. David knew what that felt like.

With Birdie standing close by, he heard her gasp. His arm went up around her shoulders, and he led her into the sitting room. It was possible Lonnie and Hal had brought reinforcements with them, but David knew it was unlikely they would do so. It would mean admitting to outsiders they'd lost their hostage. He knew it was the last thing the pair would want as they had a reputation to maintain. Even if it was only in the criminal world.

Birdie sat, and he took the nearest seat, which wasn't far away. He glanced about. The fire was burning steadily, but could use refueling. Before he did that, David wanted to ensure Birdie was calm. He reached for her hand, and she didn't deny him. Although what it really did for her, he'd never know. "The door is locked, and there are four very experienced marshals looking out for you."

Her nod was barely visible. At least David knew he'd calmed her somewhat. Well, that's what he thought anyway.

"The fire is dying down," Birdie said, her voice both quiet and wavering. David understood she was concerned but everything that could be done at this moment was already in place.

Moments later, the door handle rattled.

Birdie slapped a hand to her mouth. She was trying to stifle a scream, David was certain. He grabbed her hand and pulled her out of her chair. They ran into the kitchen.

Before he had a chance to explain, the four marshals spun around to face them. "Someone is trying to get through the front door," he explained. "I'm taking

Birdie to the root cellar. She will be safe there." He didn't give anyone a chance to respond. Instead, he pulled the kidnap victim along behind him. "I'm sorry," he told her. "It sinks like the Dickins down there."

She didn't say a word, but her expression said it all. Birdie was terrified. "I couldn't endure being held hostage again," she whispered, tears pooling in her eyes.

David completely understood. Being recaptured after escaping would have been devastating. If she was taken for a third time…it didn't bear thinking about. "You go down the ladder first," he whispered. She stared at him with those big sad eyes, and it nearly broke him. There was no choice. He had to get her out of harm's way. If they stayed put in the house, it could be a death sentence, and they both knew it.

"Will the others be alright?" she asked, her voice full of emotion.

David knew he had to be honest. It's what Birdie expected. "They are all very experienced marshals and can hold their own. The truth is, I really don't know." He waved at her to hurry down the ladder. When she was almost half way down, Birdie pulled a face. "It's overwhelming, I know," he told her, "but it's our only option." He was talking about the smell, but he could easily have been discussing the situation they found themselves in.

As soon as Birdie's feet hit solid ground, David began the climb downward. He pulled the door to the root cellar closed, and hoped the kidnappers were unable to shoot their way into the house. He hadn't heard gunshots, so for now, it seemed everyone was safe.

"What now?" Birdie asked, her face a picture of fear. Her entire body was quivering, but there was little he could do about it.

"When I bought this place, the previous owner told me something about a tunnel." David heard Birdie gulp. "Trouble is, I can't remember everything he said – it was so long ago." He shook his head in frustration.

"What sort of tunnel? Where does it lead?" Birdie demanded to know.

Running a hand through his hair, David gazed at her. "All I recall is it was used during the Indian Wars. The tunnel runs from the house to one of the old worker's cottages." He shrugged. "I guess they used it to escape if they thought they would be overrun ."

Glancing around, Birdie seemed more confused than ever, but began to pull at the shelves. "Is there a secret door?" she wondered while she continued testing.

David followed suit. Nothing budged and he believed it was simply a story from an old man with nothing better to do.

"Oh!" Birdie said, her voice wavering.

He turned in time to see one of the shelves coming toward her. Clutching the shelf, he stopped it before Birdie was hurt. "This is interesting," he said, more to himself than her. He opened it completely, waiting with baited breath for what he might find.

Right there behind the functional shelf, a doorway had been cut through, and a tunnel fashioned out of the surrounding rock. If he hadn't seen it with his own eyes, David would not have believed it.

Now it was time to find out what was at the other end.

Chapter Twenty-One

With David holding her hand, Birdie felt somewhat reassured. She took comfort in the fact he was a marshal with well over twenty years experience. He had a gun and knew how to use it, but would it be enough to keep them both safe?

She couldn't help but wonder.

"I'm not certain what we'll find at the other end," David told her, glancing back momentarily. "I was told the tunnel goes to an old worker's cottage on my property, but I have no confirmation of it. Only the ramblings of an old man."

Birdie wondered why he didn't believe the story. "If the tunnel is here as you were told, and it clearly is, why not have faith it goes to the worker's cottage?"

He turned to stare at her. "It could be true, and probably is. I just hope it's a viable situation for us." David tugged on the secret door and pulled it closed. She appreciated the fact he wouldn't assist Birdie's would-be killers to find her.

"Well, it must go somewhere," she said as she trailed behind David. "This tunnel didn't appear out of nowhere. Whoever built it would have had a destination in mind. It has to end somewhere." Or did it? What if it was abandoned before the tunnel was finished? There were piles of dirt at the sides of the tunnel, but not enough considering the size of the opening.

"I had the same thought," David said. "It must have been an escape route."

"What if there are dead bodies at the other end?" Birdie asked with a tremor in her voice.

David came to a sudden halt. "Is that what you think? You have a vivid imagination." He looked down at her, considering his next words. At least that's what it seemed like to Birdie. "There will be no bodies," he said carefully. "At worst, there would be piles of bones."

Judging by the shocked look on his face, David had heard her intake of breath. "Sorry," he mumbled. "I shouldn't have said that."

Birdie considered him for about half a minute. "Apology accepted," she finally said.

David took her hand again. "We really must go," he said, then pulled her along once more. Keeping up with his pace was not easy. He had long legs, and she didn't, but Birdie understood they needed to keep going. They also needed to do it as fast as they possibly could.

Soon they reached the end of the tunnel. There was no obvious entrance to the worker's cottage, so now they had to find a way to get inside.

~*~

Exhausted, Birdie tried to help David find a way in. Part of the issue was it was so dark. Rushing out of the ranch house as they did, neither one of them had thought to grab a lantern. They were feeling around the edges of the opening with their bare hands.

The cold did not help, and it really was cold down here. "There has to be a way in," David said, his frustration clear in his voice.

"It's like a cave," Birdie said.

"A cave," David repeated. "Could be."

Birdie could feel him moving about, but had no idea what he was doing. "You are a genius," he blurted out. "It was possibly built like a cave, with tunnels going off in different directions. Most likely to put off any Indians who found the tunnel." Moments later he lit a match. It didn't last long, but there was just enough light for them to see two additional tunnels. One to the left, and another to the right. "Which one should we take?" Birdie asked, hoping David would be more certain than she felt.

She heard him sigh. "I really have no idea. Let's try the one to the right, and if that doesn't work, we will come back and try the other one."

Her head was spinning. They were playing with their lives, but what choice did they have? David probably had a better instinct about such things than Birdie had. It meant she would go along with him. After all, what else could she do?

By the time they reached the end of the new tunnel, which thankfully was shorter than the original, her heart was racing. She could only imagine how David was feeling. He had appointed himself her personal protector, and took that responsibility seriously.

David lit another match, and the end of the tunnel lit up. But only for mere moments. "There, on the left," Birdie said urgently. "There's a…line." What that meant she really didn't know, but she truly hoped it would open so they could get to safety.

As David pushed at what she believed to be an entrance, Birdie's heartrate slowed. Were they mere minutes away from safety? And what of the marshals they'd left behind. For all she knew, they were all dead trying to save her. The thought had her light-headed.

Right on cue to pull her attention away from the negative thoughts running through her mind, Birdie heard an unfamiliar sound. A loud click and then the sound of…she wasn't sure what the second sound was.

"It's open," David whispered, "but only partially. We'll have to squeeze through." He reached for her hand, and Birdie felt his protection once again. Funny how the touch of his hand was all she needed to feel safe.

A small shard of light hit her in the face, and Birdie blanched. It had been so dark in the tunnel, they couldn't see even an inch in front of them. To say it was frightening, was an understatement.

Almost the second she was through the small gap David enticed her through, he closed the door. It was still dark in this room, but at least they had partial vision. Putting his finger to his lips, David implored her to stay quiet. After all, they didn't know exactly where they were, and who or what they might find.

He motioned at her to stay put. David opened another door, just a slither, and looked out. He stared for what seemed forever, but she knew it to be only a matter of seconds. Then he turned back to her. "Stay here," he demanded, which got her hackles up.

Since when was it alright to demand she stay put? He stared down into her face. With the little light available to them, Birdie could see the concern on his face. Instead of arguing, she nodded. He didn't need the added stress of her not complying.

David turned to walk away, then turned back again. He gazed down into her face. Without a word, he leaned in, held her tight. Then her kissed her. "I…love you," he whispered.

And then he was gone.

Chapter Twenty-Two

David didn't know what had come over him.

He was not impulsive. Never had been, but in their current situation, David wasn't sure he would ever see Birdie again. Regret had never been in his vocabulary, and he didn't intend to start now. If he hadn't told her, and he was killed trying to save her, Birdie would never know how he felt.

Cautiously, and with intent, he moved into a hallway. It was then he heard it. Someone, or something, he wasn't sure which, was nearby.

His heart fluttered with anticipation.

Hand firmly on his gun, David slowly stepped toward the sound. Then he stopped. Light surrounded him, and he blinked trying to see again. It was then he knew for certain – he was standing in the old worker's cottage. He smiled at the fast moving squirrel sitting on a dilapidated cupboard which had seen better days. The mahogany desk would have once held pride of place, and the formerly white rug had clearly been used by more than this one squirrel over the years. The broken window was partially open, and the flooring ruined.

Without a sound, he moved to the next room. This second room was clearly the kitchen. It appeared the house had been abandoned at a moment's notice. Dinner plates sat on a decaying table cloth, and remnants of food, that would have once been sustenance for the occupants, rotted as it lay where it was left. There wasn't much, only minute crumbs. The tiny creatures living here had clearly had their fill.

David checked every room, and gazed through the grubby windows to ensure they were alone. Spider webs could be found in every corner of each room. A testament of how long this building had been abandoned. After checking the other rooms, and when he was able to confirm it was safe, he returned to Birdie.

"I'm coming in," he said, pleased to be able to speak at a normal volume. "The place is a mess, but we're alone."

Birdie's relief was obvious, and she leaned into him. "I was worried about you," she whispered as her arms went up around him.

"About before," he began, but she interrupted him.

Glancing up, she smiled. "I feel the same way," she said, "but could it be because we've been forced together?"

There was always that possibility, and David knew it. Except he'd spent more than twenty years protecting women, and had never felt this way before about one of his charges. Instead of confirming either way, he put his arms around her, and held her tight. Leaning down, he kissed her like it would be the last time their lips would ever meet.

She didn't resist, nor did he expect her too. David never wanted this moment to end, except they were in a precarious situation. That part he definitely wanted to end. Birdie needed to be safe. To be free to do whatever it was she wanted. If that meant having him in her life, so be it. If she chose otherwise, that also was her choice.

His heart would shatter, he knew it would, but he would never push her into a relationship she neither wanted or asked for.

As their mouths separated, Birdie whispered, her eyes bright with unshed tears. "I love you, David. And want to spend the rest of my days with you."

Now all they had to do was get out of this alive.

~*~

He walked Birdie through the rundown cottage. It truly was a mess, but he'd expected nothing less.

There was little for them to do here, but Birdie decided to try and clean up. The chairs in the sitting room were haphazardly covered with white sheets, strangely enough. David surmised the worker's wife had thrown them on as they ran out the door.

Stranger things had been known to happen.

Birdie pulled the grubby sheets off the chairs. The sheets were covered in leaves and animal droppings. Underneath though, it was a different story. The chairs were in a relatively good condition, which meant they where able to sit and rest for a while.

It was a pity they couldn't light a fire, but it would give away their position. It was the last thing they wanted to do.

Birdie's eyes fluttered closed, but David dared not rest for even a moment. It would be easy to sleep, but their lives depended on him staying awake and alert. Everything could change in a matter of minutes.

With darkness approaching, they could find themselves in a precarious position. He couldn't hear gunfire, but David believed they were quite some distance from the main house. If it was so close they heard it, he and Birdie would be in extreme danger.

He glanced out the window as he sat next to Birdie. He needed to do another recon and ensure their safety. Birdie was now sound asleep, and he didn't want to disturb her.

David slowly stood, and his chair creaked. He watched as Birdie flinched, but she didn't awaken. Trying to get his bearings, David ambled over to the window. The moon was high in the sky, and the stars were bright. They helped him to see across the field, and it appeared free of movement. It was all he could hope for.

Glancing over at Birdie, she still slept soundly. He moved to another of the rooms and repeated the process, this time on the other side of the house. Again, there was nothing to be seen. It could be there was no threat to them here, or Lonnie and Hal had found them and were ready to pounce at the right opportunity.

David chose to believe the latter. Should he become complacent, it could mean the end of Birdie. He would not allow that to happen. Not on his watch.

As he continued to study this side of the cottage, all seemed quiet, not to mention safe. Without warning, everything changed.

In the fading light, David noticed hundreds of birds, previously pecking, searching for food, suddenly take off. There was only one reason birds did that – something or someone disturbed them.

Without hesitation, David unholstered his gun, and ran to the woman he loved. When he reached the sitting room, she was nowhere to be seen.

Chapter Twenty-Three

When a hand went around her mouth, Birdie's first impulse was to scream.

She was dragged from the chair where she slept, and pulled into another room. Her heart raced so badly, Birdie was certain she would pass out. The few words whispered in her ear changed everything. "They're all dead," Lonnie said. "We killed them all."

Glancing around the room, one thing was clear, David was nowhere to be seen. Had he been killed, like Lonnie said? Her heart pounded again, but this time it was shattered. His blood was on her hands. It was her fault – everything was her fault.

Father wanted her to travel with a bodyguard, but Birdie would have none of it. Helena wasn't a dangerous place, she'd told him repeatedly. Then suddenly it was. Her nightmare began outside one of her father's own stores. Choosing clothes for those less fortunate was one of her favorite things to do.

Birdie's charity work had always been important to her, and it was only one of the ways her family had spread their wealth around.

No matter, that life was over. More than likely, once the ransom was paid, or even before, she would be eliminated. Isn't that what Isaac and David had discussed? Her mind racing, Birdie knew it to be true.

She also knew she would not go down without a fight. The outcome would be the same, so she had nothing to lose. Without David by her side, Birdie didn't want to live. She now understood the level of grief he had suffered over the death of his wife and son. At this moment, her grief was raw and pulpable.

There was movement elsewhere in the cottage. It was slight, but it was there. Her assailant didn't seem to hear it, as he didn't react, which presented Birdie with the perfect opportunity.

Spinning around in the man's arms, her knee came up hard, connecting with his groin. The action momentarily stunned him, and he was in obvious pain. It gave her the opportunity to inflict even more pain. Birdie knew she had to act quickly while he was temporarily paralyzed by her unexpected actions.

Her arm went back, and Birdie punched the man's jaw with her fist. Her hand hurt like nothing she'd experienced before, but if he was going to kill her anyway, she would fight until the end.

As he recovered from the punch, he stared at her, his face filled with fury. Then he slapped her. Hard.

A shot rang out, and Birdie fell to the ground. It was all over. Her last thought as she fought against her closing eyes was at least she'd told David she loved him.

~*~

She awoke to chaos. Not only was David standing in front of her, but Isaac was there too.

On the floor, not far from where she sat, was a body covered in one of the sheets originally used to cover the chairs.

Several strangers moved about the room. "It's alright," David said gently. "Both Lonnie and Hal are dead."

"He shot me?" she said, not expecting her words to come out as a question.

David reached for her hand. "I shot him. You fainted. By the way, you did quite a number on him. If you hadn't fought back, I would not have gotten a clear shot."

She stared at him, not sure what to say.

"You broke his jaw with that last move. When he slapped you, it gave me a clear shot." He glanced down at her hand. The one she'd punched the killer with. "It doesn't appear broken, but we'll have the doc check it out."

"I can see Lonnie is dead, but what about Hal? You said…"

David shook his head. "Don't concern yourself. Hal is in the other room. We'll bring him in later. After we get you out of here."

"No!" she said, her heart pounding yet again. "I need to know they are no longer a threat."

Her words had shocked him. His expression told her so.

David motioned to Isaac who left the room. Moments later, Hal's body was brought in and placed beside Lonnie's.

Birdie stood, despite her light-headedness. She appreciated David putting a supporting arm around her. Together they went to where the dead men lay. Isaac pulled the sheets back from their faces.

Relief filled Birdie, and she turned to David. "Thank you," she said. "Thank you all," she said glancing at each of the marshals who were in the room. "Now I must know if my father is alright."

~*~

David arranged for Douglas Valence to be transported to Langley. The reunion of father and daughter was a tearful one, which wasn't surprising.

A quiet wedding took place less than a week later, with all Birdie's protectors, David's friends, and Birdie's father watching on.

Although her mother had passed, Birdie felt her presence and her blessing for this union.

With the previously empty bedrooms now fully furnished, Birdie's father was able to stay at the ranch house.

David had saved her life from kidnappers, but she was convinced he'd saved her in other ways. Apart from her charity work, Birdie was simply going through the motions. Now she had a purpose.

They vowed to rebuild the ranch with animals, bringing in chickens, horses, and even a cow for milk. Father was happier than she'd seen him in a long time, and Birdie was certain it was the peacefulness surrounding them.

Her abduction had taken its toll, not only on Birdie, but also her father. If she wasn't being pursued by kidnappers and murderers, Birdie knew she would have thoroughly enjoyed her time here.

Now she had a lifetime to truly enjoy her surroundings and her new husband.

Epilogue

Two years later…

David stood at the coral fence, watching the horses frolic.

Douglas Valence stood by his side. He'd never returned to Helena after he'd arrived in Langley, preferring the quiet and calmness of country life. Installing a manager to oversee his business, meant Birdie's father could live the rest of his life here, in peace. "Beautiful," Douglas said, as they watched on. A black stallion trotted over to the fence and nudged the older man, looking for treats.

David chuckled when his father-in-law reached into his pocket and pulled out an apple cut into quarters. "There you go, fella," he said, a smile on his face.

As much as they loved having Douglas there, Birdie's father was convinced he was intruding on their privacy. The compromise was to build a self-contained cottage not far from the ranch house. That way he had his privacy, and they had theirs. The construction didn't take long.

Birdie insisted Douglas join them for meals, which he happily did. "Lunch is ready," Birdie called from the top of the steps. The two men, never shying away from food, hurried inside.

Her father glanced about. "Where's Dougie," he asked, referring to his one-year-old grandson.

"He's having a nap," Birdie told him. "So I'll get to eat in peace." As much as she protested, David knew she loved that boy more than life itself. With baby number two on the way, neither would know what hit them once it arrived.

Before he sat down at the table, Douglas walked over to his daughter. "I love you," he said. "I know I don't say it enough, but I love you with all my heart."

Watching on, David couldn't help but shed a tear. There was a time he'd almost lost her. From the moment they first met, when his lips covered her mouth in that crowded church hall, he knew Birdie was his destiny.

Even surrounded by all the townsfolk, with the music and sounds of people talking and laughing, the moment was cemented in his mind.

Birdie was the one for him. Because of his actions, they would have a lifetime together.

From the Author

Thank you so much for reading my book – I hope you enjoyed it.

I would greatly appreciate you leaving a review where you purchased, even if it is only a one-liner. It helps to have my books more visible!

About the Author

Multi-published, award-winning and bestselling author Cheryl Wright, former secretary, debt collector, account manager, writing coach, and shopping tour hostess, loves reading.

She writes historical romantic suspense and historical western romance.

She lives in Melbourne, Australia, and is married with two adult children and has six grandchildren, and twin great-grandchildren.

When she's not writing, she can be found in her craft room making greeting cards.

Links

Website: *http://www.cheryl-wright.com/*

Facebook Reader Group:
*https://www.facebook.com/groups/cherylwrightaut
hor/*

Join My Newsletter:

https://cheryl-wright.com/newsletter/
(and receive a free book)

www.ingramcontent.com/pod-product-compliance
Lightning Source LLC
Chambersburg PA
CBHW070402200726
48294CB00003B/1052